THE MYSTERY OF THE GALILEAN GRINDSTONE

THE THREE INVESTIGATORS

IN

THE MYSTERY OF THE
GALILEAN
GRINDSTONE

BY

ELIZABETH ARTHUR
& STEVEN BAUER

BASED ON CHARACTERS
CREATED BY ROBERT ARTHUR

Hollow Tree Press 2025

3

A HOLLOW TREE PRESS BOOK

Copyright © 2025
Elizabeth Arthur and Steven Bauer
Hollow Tree Press LLC

Jacket Concept Elizabeth Arthur
Jacket Design and Cover Art
© 2025 Hollow Tree Press LLC
Cover Art Pashur House

"The Three Investigators" ® & "???" ®
By Permission of Elizabeth Arthur

ISBN PB: 978-1-965321-18-8
ISBN HC: 978-1-965321-19-5
ISBN EB: 978-1-965321-20-1

CONTENTS

1

A Present From Uncle Titus

Bob Andrews hopped off his bike and wheeled it along the colorfully painted seven-foot-high wooden fence surrounding the Jones Salvage Yard. His best friends Jupiter Jones and Pete Crenshaw were waiting for him to arrive with the sheaf of e-mail inquiries he'd gotten from people who hoped The Three Investigators could help them with mysteries they'd encountered. School was out and a new summer had begun. The Rocky Beach town pool was open all day, the summer league night softball games had started at the town park, and The Three Investigators were back in full-time business!

During the year, when Bob, Pete, and Jupiter had been freshmen at Rocky Beach High, they'd put their investigations on hold in order to concentrate on what was happening at school. Of course, one or two small puzzles had come their way, and they'd solved them, but mostly they'd studied.

Although the Three Investigators had always learned just as much from the work they did with their firm as they did from their classes, Rocky Beach High, unlike a lot of American schools these days, still believed in merit and competition. Or rather, its principal believed hard work should be encouraged, and that those who worked harder and did better should be rewarded.

Bob had found his science class more challenging than he'd expected, and his scientist mother had been a bit disappointed that he didn't seem likely to take after her – but he'd done well in history and English, which had made his father happy.

He'd also gotten more confident as a rock climber, and he and Mallory MacLeod, The Three Investigators' new Special Consultant, had gone climbing together four or five times in Palisade Point. Bob had also kept up with his job at the Rocky Beach Public Library – working two afternoons a week after school for the librarian, Miss Bennett.

Still, Bob couldn't have been happier that summer had come again. As he reached the end of the fence that surrounded the Salvage Yard and veered right to pass between the filigreed wrought-iron gates, he found the place humming with energy. Mathilda Jones stood on the wooden porch of the Office, shading her eyes and peering toward the entrance.

"Yoo hoo! Hello, Bob," she called, waving, and then went back to keeping a lookout.

Bob had thought he was simply arriving for the first Three Investigators' meeting of the summer, but when he saw Pete and Jupiter sitting on the edge of the porch next to Aunt Mathilda, it was clear that something else was going to happen first.

This actually didn't bother Bob. Although he'd gotten a lot of letters from prospective clients, the truth was that most of them were pretty dreary – so dreary that he'd been dreading the moment he had to share them with the others.

Now Pete and Jupiter sprang to their feet and came toward him.

"You're just in time," Pete said excitedly. "Uncle Titus and Magnus are due back from the Napa Valley at any minute, and Aunt Mathilda wants us to help unload the trucks!"

"The trucks?" Bob asked. "There's more than one?"

"Yes," Jupiter said. He looked a bit disgruntled. "My uncle and Magnus are each driving one. They've been in the Napa Valley for more than three days now, and both trucks are totally stuffed. Aunt Mathilda is afraid that

Uncle Titus may have gone overboard with his purchases."

"Maybe because Uncle Titus told her he's got a big surprise!" Pete said. "For us!"

"Where's Leif?" Bob asked, looking around him. "Is Mallory here yet?"

Magnus Haldorsson and his brother Leif were Norwegian immigrants and the Salvage Yard's resident carpenters. They were tall and blond and very good with wood. The summer before, Titus and Mathilda Jones's previous yard helpers – Bavarian brothers named Hans and Konrad – had both left to get married, and Jupiter's aunt and uncle had hired Leif and Magnus as full-time employees.

They'd also hired Mallory MacLeod as a part-time helper, and by the end of the summer, she had given The Three Investigators so much valuable help with their cases that Jupiter had asked her to join them full-time.

"Mallory's in one of the sheds," said Jupiter. "She wanted to get an hour or two of work in before our meeting – which we're obviously going to have to put off until after we unload the trucks."

"Do we have to meet in Headquarters?" Pete asked. "I vote for out here."

"I do, too," said Bob.

At the moment, Three Investigators Headquarters was an old mobile home trailer Uncle Titus had bought several years ago. When it had proved too badly damaged to sell, he'd given it to Jupiter and his friends, thinking they could find a use for it. In very short order, they'd concealed it behind piles of carefully arranged junk and had also built three secret entrances and a secret emergency exit – only one of which, Easy Three, The Three Investigators could really still use.

It was strange to consider that in only a few years all three of them had gotten too big for Tunnel Two – a length of corrugated pipe hidden behind the printing press in their outdoor workshop – and when a thief had broken in through Easy Three the previous summer, Pete, Bob, and Mallory had all started to think maybe it was time to build a new Headquarters.

Although Jupiter hadn't opposed the idea as strongly as Bob had thought he might, he hadn't been wild about it, either, and Bob wondered whether the subject would come up in their meeting this morning. It seemed likely that it would, after what both Pete and Bob had just said.

Suddenly, Bob heard three loud blasts of

an air horn, and as Aunt Mathilda started doing a little jig and jabbing her finger toward the
wrought-iron gates, Bob watched in alarm as
one of the Salvage Yard's battered old trucks
came barreling through them, followed closely
by a second one.

Boy! Bob thought. Uncle Titus is sure in
a hurry!

"Too fast, Titus," Aunt Mathilda
shrieked. "Too fast!"

Uncle Titus seemed almost to hear her –
although that was impossible, Bob thought.
The brakes locked and the truck he was driving
sprayed gravel and kicked up a cloud of dust
before coming to a halt not far from where
Bob and the others had been standing.

Magnus brought the second truck to a
more sedate stop several yards beyond where
Uncle Titus had come to rest, then hopped out,
grinning. As Uncle Titus threw open the
driver's side door of his own truck and dis-
mounted, Aunt Mathilda hurried up to him and
put her hands on her hips. She looked almost
angry.

"Titus Jones!" Aunt Mathilda said. "You
could have hurt someone!" Her cheeks were
bright red and her eyes sparked. One of her
hands flew into the air and she began wagging

a finger in his face.

"Not at all, my dear," Uncle Titus said, trying to placate her. "Not at all. I was under control at all times." He turned to Bob and the others. "Huzzah!" he said. "I knew my trusty helpers would be here. Wait 'til you see what I've brought back this time!"

"You've bankrupted us!" Aunt Mathilda said. "Two whole trucks of junk!"

"Not junk, my dear," Uncle Titus said soothingly. "Treasure."

Over the years, Bob and Pete had often helped Jupiter and his uncle unload both the marvels and the junk that Titus Jones had found on his buying trips, and Bob couldn't wait to see what he'd come back with today. He had a knack for discovering strange, weird, and unusual things. But today must be very special, Bob thought. He'd rarely seen Uncle Titus look so pleased with himself.

Now Magnus joined Uncle Titus. Bob knew that Magnus was a world-class pessimist and usually gloomy, but today even he looked cheerful and high-spirited.

"Hello, my investigating friends!" he said, smiling broadly.

Up until now, Leif had been working in the shop he shared with his brother, but on hearing the ruckus, Leif and Mallory both emerged from separate outbuildings. Leif's eyebrows and hair were coated with fine sawdust, which made him look even blonder than he actually was, while Mallory's wavy red hair shone in the sunlight like copper. She smiled and waved to Bob, and Bob felt a rush of pleasure at even just being friends with a girl like her. Bob had liked her from the moment he met her, but he liked her even more now.

In fact, if she'd been interested, he would have liked to be more than just friends with her, but it had been clear for a while now that she wanted to stick with friendship.

As Leif and Mallory joined the throng, Bob could see that Aunt Mathilda had calmed down considerably. Every now and then she dabbed at her forehead with a handkerchief or wiped a strand of her gray-brown hair out of the way, but her high color had receded and she was breathing normally.

Now she just looked like she always did when her husband had returned from one of his buying sprees – torn between believing that he'd brought back useless junk she'd never be able to sell and that he'd finally found something priceless.

"So, what do you have for me this time,

Titus?" she asked skeptically, her arms crossed on her chest.

Uncle Titus looked exuberant. "Oh, my dear," he said. "I have brought back riches that beggar description."

"That's fine, Titus," Aunt Mathilda said. "You let Mallory write the imagery and you just get this stuff unloaded."

Bob looked at Mallory, who smiled and tapped her pen on the notebook she held in her hand. She was ready to inventory everything Titus Jones had bought, and then to identify and describe the most salable items for the Salvage Yard website. Her photos and descriptions of what the Salvage Yard had for sale had been a great success, and the UPS driver, Billy Wells, now came daily to pick up packages that were being shipped to addresses all over the United States.

Magnus let down the tailgate of Uncle Titus's truck and began to unlash the covering tarpaulin, but Uncle Titus stopped him.

"Before we begin," he said, "I have something to say."

Uncle Titus loved to banter, Bob knew. He wiggled his fingers as if to begin a magic trick. He looked at the four of them, his eyes mischievous. "I have brought back something very special, something of which I'm sure you have never seen the like. Two things, actually," he said. "One of them you can touch and the other you can't."

"What are they?" Pete asked eagerly.

Uncle Titus's smile brightened. "First, Jupiter has to solve a puzzle I have for him!"

Everyone looked at Jupiter, who groaned audibly. It was an old routine of Uncle Titus's, and one Bob knew Jupiter had started to dislike. He felt he was being put on the spot like a performing seal and that such displays were beneath his dignity.

But Pete started grinning. "Come on, Jupe! You can do it. Pretend it's a game show and you're the contestant! You answer the question right and you get the prize!"

Jupiter looked at his uncle suspiciously. "Do you promise I'll be pleased with the trade?"

"I promise," Uncle Titus said, "or I'll be a monkey's uncle instead of yours."

Bob smiled. Uncle Titus also loved making jokes, and that one wasn't bad.

"So!" Uncle Titus said with brio. "I know you think you're too old for this, but this conundrum is especially for you, straight from the heart of the Napa Valley. Are you ready?"

Jupiter nodded once, if a bit moodily.

"This really happened!" Titus said. "At a vineyard in Napa where I was buying some old wine casks, there was a barrel of wine, open to the air, and the co-owners of the vineyard were arguing. One said the barrel was more than half full and the other said no, it was less than half full. How did they know who was right without measuring anything or taking any wine out of the barrel?"

Jupiter suddenly looked interested despite himself. Although Bob had had more trouble than he'd expected to in his freshman science class − a survey course that had covered physics, chemistry, and astronomy − he'd learned enough to understand that the problem related to the volume of the barrel and the volume of the wine. Still, how did you measure without measuring?

Everyone stood looking at Jupiter, and the silence got a little awkward. Jupe was thinking hard. Usually when Uncle Titus had a puzzle, Jupiter solved it in seconds to everyone's amazement. But soon enough, Jupiter spoke.

"I think," he said, "that the dispute could be settled with a simple physical maneuver. If you tilt the barrel so that the wine almost spills over the lip, then look inside, you can tell. If you can see any part of the bottom of the barrel, then it's less than half full. But if the bottom is completely covered and the wine is lapping up the side, then it's more than half full."

Since Jupiter was basically a genius – though he hated to have anyone say it – no one was at all surprised at this answer, but Uncle Titus clapped his hands in approval.

"That's my boy!" he crowed. "I knew you wouldn't let me down. The prizes will soon be yours! But you have to take possession of the one you can touch before I can tell you about the one you can't – and the first one's at the very back of the second truck."

Now everybody groaned, not just Jupiter. It wasn't, Bob knew, that they hadn't expected to work. It was that they hadn't expected to have to completely clear both of the trucks out before they could see whatever Uncle Titus had found, and bought, and brought back to them.

Even so, everyone moved forward, ready to begin, until Uncle Titus raised his two hands, palms outward.

"Now let's be organized about this. Mallory, I see you're ready to take inventory. Boys, don't walk away without making sure Mallory has written down whatever you're carrying.

18

And since by this time she knows where everything is in this whole dang place, she'll tell you
where to put it so that it's like with like."

Though it was just the middle of the
morning, the day was already heating up and
sweat trickled down Bob's neck. As they began
to work, Aunt Mathilda hurried to the house
and returned with pitchers of lemonade and ice
water.

"Drink, drink!" she kept exhorting.
"Don't get dehydrated!"

Bob was amazed at the variety of stuff
Uncle Titus had discovered. There were used
oak wine casks, empty bottles of various shapes
and colors, antique corkscrews, stained glass,
Victorian architectural doodads. There was a
solid mahogany door, a porcelain sink, two
leaded glass sidelights, and a whole bunch of
things even Mallory didn't seem to have names
for yet.

When Aunt Mathilda wasn't urging peo-
ple to drink, she was *oohing* and *ahhing* over her
husband's finds. Every now and then she would
frown in dismay about something she was sure
they'd never sell, but in general she seemed to
approve of his choices. Her anxiety evapo-
rated. Perhaps they wouldn't go bankrupt after
all!

Her favorite new item was a winged marble angel that had stood in an elaborate Victorian garden. There were other garden ornaments of marble and metal, carvings of squirrels and rabbits, garden globes and gazing orbs, tall obelisks for climbing vines, and several fancy trellises and arbors.

It seemed to Bob that the trucks were like that chest of wonders in the fairy tale that you could never empty, no matter how much you took out. But when they were almost empty, Titus clapped his hands, calling everyone to attention. Bob was glad to take a break. He was a bit woozy from the heat and hard work. In fact, he was almost wishing that he and the others had picked a different day for their first Three Investigators meeting of the summer!

"All right, you four," Uncle Titus said, looking from Bob to Mallory to Pete to Jupiter. "You've fulfilled your end of the bargain admirably. Jupiter solved the puzzle, and you've all worked your butts off."

"Titus!" Aunt Mathilda said.

"It's O.K.," Pete reassured her. "We've heard worse."

"I told you I'd brought you something special," Uncle Titus said. "And I have.

Magnus?"

"Come on, Leif," Magnus said to his brother. The two of them jumped up into the bed of the truck and began wrestling with something flat and heavy on a tarpaulin. They dragged it to the edge of the truck and then struggled to set it carefully on the ground.

It was a circular stone disk about two and a half feet in diameter and three inches thick. It had a rectangular hole in the middle, from which a hairline crack ran almost to the edge.

"It's a grindstone!" Uncle Titus said. "A real, old-fashioned grindstone – the kind that knife grinders would hang on a frame and turn with pedals. I found it in an outbuilding of a most unusual house – or rather a castle – in the Napa Valley."

"Is that a crack?" Aunt Mathilda said, tilting her glasses and looking closely.

"Yes, my dear," Titus said.

"And who do you think will buy an old-fashioned grindstone with a crack?" Aunt Mathilda asked, her voice sharp.

"No one will buy it," Titus said. "Because I'm giving it to Jupiter and his friends – as a memento of a case they haven't solved yet!"

A shiver ran up Bob's spine. Wow! he thought. He knew how seriously Jupiter's uncle took their investigative firm, and if he thought this grindstone might lead to a case, it probably would.

"You can't see them now," Uncle Titus added, "but on the other side of the grindstone someone has carved letters and numbers into the stone. They've been eroded over time, but you can still see them, and I think that's fairly strange, don't you?"

"Where did you get the stone?" Bob asked. "And why do you think it could lead to a new case?"

Uncle Titus cleared his throat. "We were at a winery in the Napa Valley – the one where I got the puzzle! – and the owners suggested we stop by a nearby house that had recently been bought by a couple from Portugal. They said the house had always been called a "castle" – even though it wasn't made of stone, but of wood – and that the new owners were renovating it. I took the advice I'd been given and met Felix and Fortunata Serreno. They came to the United States to study hotel management, but after they got jobs here, they stayed. A charming couple! They have a toddler and Fortunata is pregnant again.

"They bought the so-called castle about four months ago," Uncle Titus went on. "It's a most unusual place. The Serrenos plan to turn it into a small hotel. The grindstone came from an outbuilding they were cleaning out so that some stonemasons could stay there while they restore some of the damaged stone features on the grounds. The previous owner didn't really keep the place up."

"Why did you say the house was so unusual?" asked Mallory. "And why is it called a castle?"

"It's a high Victorian house," Uncle Titus said. "The sort of house you see in San Francisco, but bigger. It's quite a sight, sitting tucked near the mountains at the southern part of the Napa Valley. It was built in the 1880s, the Serrenos told me. And it's – a calendar house!"

"A calendar house?" Mallory exclaimed. "My parents took me to see one once, in the Orkney Islands, in northern Scotland. The one I saw had a secret passage behind the bookcases in the library. I loved it."

"Why are they called calendar houses?" Pete asked.

"Guess!" said Uncle Titus. "Well, don't guess. Because, according to the Serrenos, their house has twelve exterior doors for the twelve months of the year, fifty-two rooms for the weeks, seven turrets for the number of days in a week, and three-hundred-sixty-five panes of glass – one for each day in the year. Isn't that something?"

"Fifty-two rooms!" Pete said. "The place must be gigantic!"

"Some of the rooms are very small, I think," Uncle Titus said. "More like closets. And a lot of the windows have multiple panes of glass. The house isn't really as big as it sounds. Still, it's quite impressive." He paused and looked at them teasingly. "Though when the Serrenos bought it, they hadn't heard the rumors!"

"The rumors?" asked Pete excitedly.

"Yes, indeed," Uncle Titus said. "The rumor is that there's a treasure hidden somewhere in the house – or maybe in the grounds!"

"Titus Jones," Aunt Mathilda said severely. "Now don't go filling these impressionable heads with your twaddle."

"Twaddle!" Uncle Titus said. "I take that very much amiss."

"A hidden treasure!" Pete said. "What kind?"

"Your guess is as good as mine," said

Uncle Titus. "But I told the Serrenos that my nephew was the head of an investigative firm, and although they didn't hire you on the spot, when I told them you'd discovered a stash of gold hidden for over a hundred years, they *did* seem interested in your past accomplishments!"

The summer before, Bob, Pete, and Jupiter had solved six challenging cases in less than three months, but the one in which they'd found the gold had gotten them the most attention, and since it had been the first case Bob had written up and posted on The Three Investigator's new website, it had also started Bob off on a new branch of his work as Records and Research – writing up their cases and posting the write-ups online.

"Did you give Mr. and Mrs. Serreno one of our cards?" asked Pete. Pete had an almost mystical belief that once a Three Investigators card had been bestowed, a case was sure to follow.

"I didn't have any to give," Uncle Titus said. "And since they only bought the house four months ago, they're not really open for business yet. Even so, you might want to get yourselves up to the Napa Valley sometime this summer to see what you can find out. In the meantime, let's get this grindstone to wherever you want us to put it, Jupiter. After that, you can put your nose to it!"

That was a truly good joke, Bob thought, as everyone laughed with Uncle Titus. But although Uncle Titus had suggested that they might get up to the Napa Valley sometime this summer, Bob was suddenly filled with a desire to go at once.

After all, even though The Three Investigators didn't normally just spring off into the blue to poke around in a place where there were vague rumors of treasure, as far as Bob could remember, Uncle Titus had never attempted to interest The Three Investigators in a case before.

In addition, if someone associated with the calendar house had taken the trouble to engrave a simple grindstone with symbols or letters, Bob had to wonder why. Craftspeople sometimes decorated tools to make them beautiful as well as useful, but a grindstone seemed an oddly utilitarian thing to decorate.

As for the rumors about hidden treasure, although in Bob's experience rumors like that were frequently all smoke and no fire, the fact that Felix and Fortunata Serreno hadn't known there even *were* such rumors before they bought their new house seemed to make it more likely

that there was at least a bit of a fire somewhere. If so, then maybe this grindstone really
would be a memento of a case The Three Investigators hadn't solved yet!

2

Some Very Intriguing Symbols

Although Jupiter still felt a little winded from the effort of helping his uncle unload the heavily loaded trucks, as he stared down at the grindstone Leif and Magnus had just deposited at the edge of the outdoor workshop, he was happy to finally have the chance to see the stone right-side up – with the marks his uncle had described plainly visible.

There were four symbols that looked like moons surrounded by a circle, and a triangle with a C or a G – or maybe an O – in the middle. The grindstone itself was yellowish-white and looked rather soft, and since the letters and numbers had a blurred look about them, Jupiter thought it was probably sandstone, which had been left in the rain over the years.

So far, there was nothing particularly exciting about this stone, Jupiter thought. Of course, it *was* a bit strange that anyone would have taken the time and trouble to carve it, but even together with rumors of hidden treasure, he hardly thought it would warrant a trip all the way to the Napa Valley. He moved around the stone to get a better look at it, and as he did, Pete dropped to his knees and shoved his face as close to the stone as he could.

"I'm doing just what your uncle said we should do," he explained. "Putting my nose to the grindstone. I can see the marks, but I can't figure out what they are." He sat back up. "Where did that expression about putting your nose to the grindstone come from, anyway?"

Since no one else seemed able to answer, and since Jupiter had seen photographs of men using these grindstones in the old days, he said, "You have to imagine the stone sitting upright in a wooden casement. The knife-grinder bent over the stone as he pedaled to set the wheel spinning, then held the blade to be sharpened against its spinning edge, probably bringing his face quite close. In those days, knife grinding was hard labor."

"Everything was hard labor in those days," said Mallory. "Including inscribing these symbols. Why do you think someone did it? And what *is* that letter in the middle of the triangle?"

Though Jupiter was feeling acutely aware that today marked a whole new era in the history of The Three Investigators – the day when a Special Consultant officially joined their firm, at his specific invitation – and he was also trying to suppress a desire to second-guess that decision, he bent down to feel the edges of the grindstone and studied the letter carefully.

"I think it's a G," he reported. "And I wouldn't exactly call what surrounds it a triangle."

"Yes, it is!" Pete said. "Though the edges seem a lot thicker than they need to be."

"That's what I meant," said Jupiter. "Also, although the outside edges are straight, there's a sort of inward-jumping notch halfway down the left and right sides."

"You're right," Bob said. "And that circular symbol at the top isn't simple, either. Although the four inner circles look like moons of different sizes, the big circle holding them looks like it has rays shooting outward from its edge."

Jupiter looked at it again and saw what Bob meant. It seemed as if someone had tried to carve the rays of a corona into the stone. When he, Bob, and Pete had been in fourth grade, their teacher had taken them on a field trip to see a total eclipse of the sun, and Jupiter had never forgotten the sight of the sun's rays flaring out all around the black disc of the moon.

"It almost looks like a rendering of a total eclipse of the sun," Jupiter observed, finally starting to get interested in the puzzle. "If that's what it really is, those discs could be moons imposed on a moon's shadow."

"And the moons could be the four original moons of Jupiter," Mallory said, only half-joking. "Io, Europa, Ganymede, and Callisto."

"Your satellites!" Pete said to Jupiter, grinning. Though Jupiter, too, knew the names of the original moons of Jupiter, he wasn't sure that Pete did.

Still, the motive for Pete's comment was a kind one – he was reminding Jupiter and the others of their discovery the summer before that Jupiter's parents had named him Jupiter because they'd both been astronomers.

By now, Pete was down on his knees again, running his hands over the markings.

"What do you think these letters in the middle are?" he added. "One of them looks like either a C or G again, and three of them are either Ls or Is."

"Why don't we take a rubbing?" Mallory asked. "Aside from the rain damage, it's also hard to see the surface clearly in the sunlight. A rubbing would sort it out."

Pete asked, "What's a rubbing?"

Mallory looked at the three of them a bit skeptically.

"Are you three trying to tell me you've never done a rubbing? I used to do them all the time in Scotland," she said. "On gravestones. We'd take a big piece of paper, lay it on the stone, then rub over it with a piece of charcoal. Where there's an indentation, the charcoal skips over it, and it reads as white space."

Although Jupiter had never heard of this technique as a formal practice, the minute Mallory described it, he realized that almost everyone must have done it, informally, at some point in their lives.

So did Bob – who said, "Let's do it! We have a pad of extra-large paper in Headquarters left over from that history project we did a couple of years ago, and I think there's some charcoal, too, from Halloween."

"Go get whatever we've got," Jupiter told him – at which Bob made a dash for Easy Three and Headquarters. Soon he was back with a big piece of thin white paper and a stick of soft charcoal, both perfect for the job at hand.

Unfortunately, he also came back with

an observation Jupiter wasn't sure he wanted to hear.

"Boy, that trailer seems to get smaller all the time," he said. "Mallory was on to something when she said we'd outgrown it."

Jupiter couldn't help but remember, when Bob said this, that toward the end of the summer before, Mallory — who had first seen The Three Investigators' inner sanctum the day it was broken into by a robber — had observed that Headquarters was crowded, messy, and too small for the boys' current needs.

But although Jupiter had been — reluctantly — willing to consider letting go of their old Headquarters and building a new one, until Bob brought it up today, no one had mentioned it for many months.

Now, however, they were all mentioning it at the same moment.

"Bob's right, Jupiter," Pete said. "It's not getting any bigger."

"Unlike the universe," Mallory said, "which is expanding all the time."

"There may be something in what you're all saying," Jupiter said, a bit unwillingly. "But for now, let's concentrate on the task at hand."

With that, Bob dropped to his knees, spread the paper over the grindstone, and made a tentative motion with the charcoal.

"Is this how you do it?" he asked Mallory.

"Yes," she said. "Someone else should hold the paper steady."

Pete did as she'd suggested, but although Bob rubbed as vigorously as he could, for a minute or two he produced nothing but a uniform light gray.

At last, the white edge of the circle at the top became visible, and as Jupiter looked at it, he thought it *did* seem to have rays like the rays of a corona carved around it. The moons inside it looked even more like moons on the rubbing than they did to the naked eye.

With the top of the grindstone successfully rubbed, Bob moved to the bottom – where soon it was evident that the letter in the center of the triangle *was* a G, and that, just like the circle, the triangle was more detailed and complex than it seemed to need to be.

As Jupiter stared at what the rubbing had revealed, he thought he might have seen something like it before somewhere, but since he couldn't think where, he didn't mention it, and Bob moved to the center of the grindstone.

There, numbers began to appear as white spaces on the paper. The number 2 was followed by a 4, and then a 6 and a 1.

"Even numbers," Bob said, "until we get to the 1. No pattern there."

But left to right, Jupiter saw, was the number 1642, which looked a lot like a date, he thought.

His hunch was soon proved correct as Bob went on, revealing an O, an I, an A, an N – and soon it read GENNAIO 1642.

"That looks like Italian," Bob observed. "And if it's a month, it probably begins with a J in English – which means January, June, or July." Of the possibilities, January seemed the most probable to Jupiter.

"Keep going, Bob," Pete said. "You're on a roll."

And so the next month and year were revealed, until the inscription read 15 FEBBRAIO 1564 – 8 GENNAIO 1642. It was pretty clear that the first month was February.

"Look," Pete said, pointing. "We learned last summer that Europeans put the day before the month."

"Yes," said Jupiter. "Even though this isn't a gravestone but a grindstone, that looks a lot like the dates of someone's life."

"But what's it doing in California?" Pete said. "There were only tribes of Native Americans in the 1600s – and maybe a conquistador or two."

"Hold on," Bob said. "I'll do the other marks."

As he worked briskly across the center of the grindstone, more letters came into view as white spaces on the gray background.

I, E, L, I, L, A, G.

He sped up across the rest of the letters and stood up triumphantly when they could all see that the words read GALILEO GALILEI.

"Galileo!" Bob exclaimed. "We learned in science class that he's the one who discovered the four moons of Jupiter, so maybe the G in the triangle at the bottom is the first letter of both of his names!

"A very reasonable hypothesis," Jupiter said.

"If this is a kind of gravestone for Galileo, it sure seems weird to find it in California," Pete said.

"It *does* seem weird," Mallory agreed. "Maybe your uncle was onto something when he said this might be a memento of a case we haven't solved yet. A case about Galileo! You'd like that, wouldn't you, Jupiter? After all, Galileo invented the scientific method!"

"That's true," Jupiter said. "He came up

with hypotheses and then tried to disprove them. If he did, he re-thought them and tried again."

"But Galileo was Italian," Pete said. "Wasn't he born in Pisa?"

"I think that's right," Mallory said.

"I remember that he got in a lot of trouble with the Catholic Church," Bob said, "for saying that the earth circled the sun and not the other way around."

"That's correct," Jupiter said. "Before Galileo did his experiments, Nicolaus Copernicus published a book that argued that the sun was at the center. But Galileo was the one who actually proved that heliocentrism, not geocentrism, was right."

"But the Catholic Church made him take it back," Mallory said. "He had to recant to save himself. Even so, he spent the rest of his life under house arrest."

"Yes," Jupiter said. "Though if I'm remembering correctly, he recanted his recantation. The Catholic Church made him say that the earth stood still − at the center of the universe. But after his trial he said, 'And yet it moves.'"

"My parents are Catholic," Pete said, "but I thought that was totally great. That he stuck to his guns about what he knew he'd found out."

"It *was* great," said Bob. "Still, the real question at the moment is why did a Californian in the Napa Valley carve Galileo's name and dates of birth and death on a grindstone? And why did they add the symbols of moons and triangles and coronas and so on? I don't know about the rest of you, but I'm getting excited by both the grindstone and the rumors about hidden treasure. In fact, I think we should consider taking your uncle's advice and going up to the Napa Valley to poke around."

Jupiter looked at Bob in surprise. "But I thought you told me you were really pleased with some of the e-mail inquiries the firm has gotten recently. That you were sure we'd really like them."

"I lied," Bob said.

"Hmm," said Jupiter, "that's disappointing. But it's six hours to the Napa Valley, and we don't know anyone we can stay with. My uncle said that Castello Serreno isn't open for business yet, and even if it were, there's no real reason to imagine that there would be anything to discover if we *did* find a place to stay."

"There was no real reason to imagine that the rumors about Li Chang's gold were true, either," Bob said, "but in the end, we found it. Why couldn't that be true this time, too?"

"I suppose it could," said Jupiter thoughtfully.

"One thing's for sure," Mallory said. "Since Bob's been giving alphabetical titles to our cases, *whatever* case ends up being the first one this summer, it'll use the letters GG — and if this is the case, Bob will already have his title!"

"That's right!" Pete said. "It'll be *The Mystery of the Galilean Grindstone*! Oh, come on, Jupiter, let's do it! For Bob!"

"Don't do it for me," said Bob, looking a bit alarmed. "I wouldn't want to be responsible for dragging all of you up to the Napa Valley just to have us discover nothing at all. Of course, it would be great if we could solve a case that already had a title and a memento before we even started, but that's not the way things normally work in life. Also, given how bad I am at science, I have trouble believing that I'm destined to write about a case featuring Galileo."

"Not Galileo, necessarily," said Mallory. "But somebody who was interested in him, or admired him for some reason. Why don't we sit down for a minute so I can see whether Castello Serreno has a website?"

As Pete sat in one of the metal chairs in the outdoor workshop and Mallory sat in another, Bob and Jupiter went to stand behind her while she booted up her laptop.

"How do you spell 'Serreno'?" she asked. "One r or two?"

"I'd try two," Bob suggested. "And plug in Napa Valley."

Mallory typed for a minute and then pressed ENTER.

"Here we go," she said as she looked at the list of search results. "There's a website for a Castello Serreno in the southern part of the Napa Valley."

She clicked on the link, a window opened up, and Jupiter found himself looking at an enormous Victorian house with several stories, many turrets and towers, different roof pitches, and what looked like lots and lots of windows.

COMING SOON, the banner headline read.

A UNIQUE BOUTIQUE HOTEL. CASTELLO SERRENO! PUT A FUTURE VISIT ON YOUR CALENDAR!

Jupiter could see that this was still a website in progress as Mallory clicked on several of the links in the menu. The link for "Accommodations" led to a page that read UNDER CONSTRUCTION. But the link for HISTORY had several paragraphs. Jupiter tried to read them but the words were small enough and far enough away that he could only pick out some of them.

"It says that the house was built in 1880 by a rich Italian immigrant," Mallory said. "His name was Giuseppe Donati. He'd gone bankrupt back in Italy, where he'd hired a famous architect to build him a gigantic and very elegant house – a house that burned down. And guess what? That house was in Pisa. In America, Donati made a fortune in Napa Valley wines, and although he spent a lot of it building the house the Serrenos have just bought, he gave some of it to a Franciscan monastery that had fallen on hard times."

"This guy Donati was from Pisa?" Pete asked. "Well, that proves it, doesn't it? That he was the one who carved the symbols on the grindstone?"

"It doesn't exactly prove it," said Jupiter. "But it does suggest it." And for the first time since his uncle had mentioned the grindstone, Jupiter began to wonder if there really might be something to investigate at Castello Serreno.

Mallory clicked on a live link in the HISTORY text, and was taken to a section called ACTIVITIES NEAR CASTELLO SERRENO.

"It seems the monastery is still there," she reported. "It's tucked into the foothills of the mountains, not far from the castle, and the Serrenos suggest that their future guests might want to go and see it. They also suggest a visit to a small astronomical observatory perched on a hillside in the mountains. It's owned by the monastery."

There was another link, and when Mallory clicked on it, she was taken to photographs of both the monastery and the observatory. When she enlarged them, Jupiter saw an elegant and classical old stone building with arches and a small round observatory.

"Look!" Mallory said. "The monastery has a guest house with guest rooms!"

"Maybe we could stay *there*!" Pete said. "If Worthington could drop us off, we could use our bikes to get back and forth between the calendar house and the monastery!"

"If we can get reservations, that might work very well," Jupiter said.

Then Mallory clicked on the page about the observatory.

There were close-ups of some of the exterior features, and as Mallory enlarged a photograph of its front entrance, Jupiter saw that just above the door a round block of stone had been set, on which was inscribed a strangely thick-sided equilateral triangle with a G in its center.

"Look at that!" Bob exclaimed.

"Good grief, it's the symbol on the bottom of the grindstone!" Mallory said.

It was, too – although this time it was clearly visible – and as Jupiter stood and stared at it, he knew that if they could arrange it, he and the others would soon be departing for the Napa Valley. There were clearly mysteries to untangle.

After all, even though Giuseppe Donati would have hired an architect to design his new American house, from the evidence of the symbol on both the grindstone and the doorway of the astronomical observatory, it would seem that the same architect had designed both the observatory and Castello Serreno.

If that was what had happened, Jupiter reflected, then it was entirely possible that there was more of a connection between the Franciscan monastery and Giuseppe Donati than might be evident at first glance. If they could stay at the monastery, it might give them some sort of special access to the history of the relationship between the two buildings.

In a way, Jupiter thought, it was exceedingly strange that a Franciscan monastery had built an astronomical observatory at all. He was just about to say this when he decided, instead, to suggest that they continue their investigation inside Headquarters. After all, even if his friends were right that it was time for them to build a new one, at the moment, the old mobile home trailer was all they had – and truth to tell, Jupiter was very fond of it!

A Disagreeable Visit

As Pete settled himself in Headquarters, he watched Bob shove some stuff around on the crowded desk and boot up the firm's ancient desktop computer – only to find that there really *wasn't* anywhere else to stay close enough to bike to and from the calendar house except for the Franciscan monastery. That was fine with Pete, since the main thing he was hoping was that all of them would be heading for the Napa Valley soon. He thought staying in a monastery while they were there sounded pretty cool.

Pete had thought Bob really wanted to go, too, but then Bob had said that stuff about not wanting to be responsible for dragging all of them up to the Napa Valley just to have them discover nothing. Jupiter clearly also had his doubts about just pushing off to some big old Victorian house on a treasure hunt, so Pete didn't want to seem silly by showing wild enthusiasm for the idea.

Even so, he *was* enthusiastic. Very. In fact, he couldn't think of a better way to start the summer than to head off on a road trip to a place he'd never been before, in the company of his best friends.

Perched uncomfortably on a folding chair, with groaning shelves close behind him and a pile of books to his right, Pete couldn't help but think again that Bob had been right when he'd commented on how small Headquarters was getting. It would be a lot of fun to get out in the open somewhere.

As Bob got up the monastery's website, he paused and turned to Jupiter. "Maybe we should call the Serrenos first to make sure they wouldn't object to us showing up to try and find their hidden treasure."

"From what my uncle said, I'm sure they wouldn't," Jupiter said. "Not that it's the hidden treasure we're really interested in, of course."

"It isn't?" Pete exclaimed. What was Jupiter talking about?

"Not really," Jupiter said. "After all, if we were to find something valuable in the house or grounds, it wouldn't belong to us. It would belong to the Serrenos. Of course, it's always exciting to discover something that's been hidden, but even though we've sometimes gotten rewards when we've done that, with most of our cases, solving the mystery was all we ever really wanted."

"That's true," Bob said. "And right now, the thing *I'd* really like to know is why an astronomical observatory owned by Franciscan monks has the same symbol on it that's on a grindstone your uncle found at a nearby calendar house!"

Pete didn't disagree with that, but thought Bob had it backwards. *He* wanted to know why the calendar house had had a Galilean grindstone stored in one of its outbuildings to begin with.

Bob clicked on a link to the monastery's reservations site, but as he filled in dates on the reservations calendar, his voice swelled with disappointment. "Oh, no! Starting in just eight days, all the rooms in the guest house are filled for a month." Bob reset the dates, then said, "Still, as of now, there are four cells available."

"Cells?" Pete exclaimed. "I thought cells were for prisoners!"

"They can be," said Jupiter. "But the word *cell* merely means a small room – one in which a prisoner is locked up or in which a monk or nun sleeps. Or the smallest structural and functional unit of an organism, of course."

Pete, Bob, and Mallory all laughed, then

looked at the photographs of the guest rooms in the Mountain Monastery.

In a way, they were plain and even stark – with crosses on the walls above the beds – but they all had long, tall windows looking out on well-watered grounds, and they all had a bed, a washstand, a bureau, and a chair next to a little desk.

Although Pete's parents were Catholic, and so were his many cousins and aunts and uncles, Pete knew almost nothing about monasteries or convents. Still, he thought the rooms looked nice, and when another link led to a photograph of something called a "refectory" – a big room in the main monastery where the monks took their meals with their guests – that looked really great.

"Shall I make some reservations?" Bob asked. "For the day after tomorrow, maybe? Or should we call Worthington first to see if he can take us then?"

Mallory started to say something in response, but before she could get her words out, Bob said suddenly, "Oh, no! It says here that they don't have Wi-Fi – at least not available to the guests. We could live with that, I guess, but they also don't allow girls or women to stay in the guest house. They can go to the services, but not stay overnight. We'll have to find somewhere else to stay."

Pete was surprised at how disappointed he felt – though he felt embarrassed at his disappointment. After all, it wasn't Mallory's fault that she was a girl!

However, Mallory said, "Don't worry. I won't be able to come with you, anyway. My father's first cousin invited me and my mother to visit him this weekend. He lives in Vancouver, British Columbia, and we already have our tickets. I'm sure they can't be changed."

"Maybe not," Bob said, "but I can't believe that any monastery would ban girls from its guest house. This isn't the Dark Ages, for heaven's sake."

"I can't believe it, either," Pete said indignantly. Still, secretly, he felt relieved at the ease with which the problem had been solved – although he was also truly sorry Mallory wouldn't be coming with them.

"Even if you *won't* be coming with us, I don't think they should have rules like that," he said. "What if they didn't allow people named Jones or Andrews to stay there? You can't just turn people away for whatever-they're-called reasons!"

"Arbitrary?" asked Bob.

"Yes, arbitrary!" Pete agreed.

Mallory smiled. "That's nice of you, Pete," she said, "but I actually think the monastery has a right to make whatever rules they want to. After all, it's a private organization and, let's face it, the men are monks."

"Are you sure you wouldn't mind if we stayed there?" Bob asked.

"Of course I'm sure," Mallory said. "Since I can't go, anyway, what difference does it make?"

Pete still felt a bit confused and more than a little guilty. His reaction to the news that the monastery didn't let women stay there had been far less vehement than Bob's – perhaps because he was fascinated by the idea of staying at the monastery himself. What would it be like? Would there be a lot of praying at dinner? Would everyone be wearing robes and sandals? Would there be incense and chanting?

Even so, he was truly disappointed to learn that Mallory wouldn't be coming with them to the Napa Valley. She had great ideas and a lot of energy, and besides, she'd already been to a calendar house and knew something about them. He bet she was unhappy that she wouldn't get to see another one.

"Wouldn't you like to see Castello

50

Serreno?" he asked curiously.

"I'd love to," said Mallory. "And if there's any way I can get up to the Napa Valley after I get back from Canada, I'll do it. But for now, I think we should see if we can find out more about the history of these buildings."

Just then, Bob said, "Wow, look at this. It's an article about a calendar house in Austria. It's called Schloss Eggenberg, and it was built during a time when the calendar itself was in dispute. You know the Gregorian calendar? The one we use now? Apparently it was invented in 1582 and approved by a pope called Pope Gregory. It says that the earlier calendar – the Julian calendar, originated by Julius Caesar – wasn't very exact, and by Pope Gregory's time, the earth, in its orbit, was about ten days ahead of itself.

"So Pope Gregory proposed doing away with ten days in October of 1582, and October 4th was followed by October 15th. It says that because of the changes in the calendar, the Schloss Eggenberg architect tried to cover all the bases – whether you wanted a month with 31, 30, 29, or 28 days. He also went so far as the number of hours in the day and even the number of minutes in an hour."

"Wait a minute," Pete said. "You mean

that this Pope Gregory guy just got rid of ten whole days? Just whisked them out of existence, as if he were a wizard? What about the people who had birthdays during the days he magicked away?"

When everyone laughed uproariously at this comment, Pete said, "Well, I mean it. Even though my birthday *does* happen to be in October, it doesn't seem very scientific to simply *erase* ten days that people might have plans for. Not just birthdays, but other things, too."

"Pete's right," Mallory said. "It must have been very inconvenient and upsetting to suddenly have your schedule so drastically rearranged. But it wasn't unscientific. Just the opposite in fact. Science is about discovering the order that rules the cosmos. In fact, on our tour of Balfour Castle we learned that by building a calendar house, an architect thought he was creating something in tune with the order of the cosmos."

"That's what it says here, too," Bob reported. "And you know, I just realized something. Galileo was born in 1564, which means he was just eighteen years old when Pope Gregory reformed the calendar. I bet that made a big impression on him. Maybe it affected him enough so that he became a person

who could prove that heliocentrism – not geocentrism – was correct, when he grew up."

"If so," Jupiter said, "it's a bit ironic that
the very same church that inspired Galileo to
become a scientist also punished him for his
discoveries. Anyway, I've been thinking. Even
though the Mountain Monastery must be a lot
older than the calendar house, the observatory
must have been built at the same time as the
Serranos' hotel. And from the evidence of the
stone over the observatory door, I'd posit that
the two buildings were designed by the same
architect."

When Jupiter said this, Pete suddenly remembered something Charlotte Mitchell had
said about her aunt, Phillipa Paxton.

Pete, Bob, and Jupiter had met Dr. Paxton on their second investigation of the previous
summer, and they'd all ended up really liking
her. She was from Wyoming, and even though
she was a history professor at the same college
where Bob's mother taught science, she liked to
wear cowboy clothes, and Pete had sometimes
thought that she and The Three Investigators'
old mentor, Mr. Sebastian, might get along.
Hector Sebastian was currently living in Wyoming, but only for a year or two, after which
he'd be back in California.

"I wonder if Phillipa Paxton would know anything about them," Pete said. "The last time I talked to Charlotte Mitchell, she told me her aunt was working on a new book about California in the 19th century – a book about old buildings and the people who built them."

"Indeed?" said Jupiter, looking at Pete with interest. "Maybe Bob should call her and ask if we can meet with her tomorrow."

But though Bob tried both of Phillipa Paxton's landlines – the one at her house and the one at Reedmore College – he got voice-mail recordings on both of them.

"I'll try her again later," he said.

"When you say she's working on a book about old buildings and the people who built them, do you mean the architects or the owners?" Mallory asked Pete.

"I don't know," Pete said. "Maybe both. Don't architects and home owners usually work pretty closely together?"

"It depends on the architect, I think," Mallory said. "Whoever designed the calendar house in the Napa Valley must have worked pretty closely with Giuseppe Donati, but the house where my mother and I live was proba-bly designed by someone who just liked the Vic-torian style."

"That's right," Bob said. "The Wessex House is a Victorian, too."

"And luckily, when they broke it up into apartments, they didn't ruin it," Mallory said.

"Is your mother still looking for another place to live?" Bob asked curiously.

"When our house in Scotland finally sold, she did look for a little while," Mallory said, "but since houses here are much more expensive than houses in Scottish towns, luckily, she's given up – at least for now."

"Why luckily?" asked Pete.

"Because I'm really picky about houses, and I'd much rather live in the Wessex House than most of the houses being built in California these days," Mallory said. "I love old buildings, and I've sometimes thought I'd like to be an architect myself. I design buildings on graph paper all the time."

Pete suddenly found himself saying something very unexpected. "If you like designing buildings, maybe you could design a new Three Investigators Headquarters!"

But just as Mallory, Bob, and Jupiter all turned to look at him, surprised expressions on their faces, the phone suddenly rang.

"Three Investigators Headquarters," Jupiter said, as he punched the speakerphone button.

"Is that Jupiter? This is Phillipa Paxton. I've just gotten back to my house, and I saw on Caller I.D. that The Three Investigators had called. What's up? Are you on a new case?"

"We may be," Jupiter said. "But we need more information before we can know for sure, and Pete learned from Charlotte that you're working on a book about 19th-century California buildings."

"That's true," said Dr. Paxton. "I plan to have sections about buildings in all the major regions of the state."

"Including the Napa Valley?" Jupiter asked.

"Including the Napa Valley," Dr. Paxton said.

"Do you know anything about a big Victorian built in the 1880s near a Franciscan monastery in the foothills of the southern mountains?" Jupiter asked. "The house was built by an Italian named Giuseppe Donati. We understand he made a fortune in wines and gave some of it to the monastery, though the mystery we may be investigating would be at the Victorian − now a hotel called Castello Serreno."

Dr. Paxton's voice grew thoughtful.

"How interesting," she said. "Although I haven't actually researched either building yet, I've tabbed some research sites, and I'll be happy to do some preliminary work to see what might pop up. If the three of you want to come to my house tomorrow afternoon, I can see you at 2:00."

When Dr. Paxton said "the three of you," Pete shot a glance at Mallory. He was glad when Jupiter said, "There would actually be four of us. Mallory MacLeod has joined the firm as a Special Consultant. It was Mallory who identified the supposed Jessie Frémont replica quilt in Lyle Smith's collection as the original."

"Of course!" said Dr. Paxton. "I met her at the opening in San Francisco. By all means, the four of you, then."

"We'll see you at 2:00," said Jupiter. He hung up the phone and nodded. "Well, *that* worked out well," he said. "Now let's get reservations for the three of us at the Franciscan monastery and hope that Worthington can drive us to the Napa Valley the day after tomorrow."

A short while later, after Bob had reached Worthington and he'd said he could take them, an e-mail confirming their reservations at The St. Francis Mountain Monastery was deposited in The Three Investigators In-box.

Pete was about to return to the subject he had broached before Dr. Paxton called – the subject of having Mallory design The Three Investigators a new Headquarters – when the intercom squawked. Aunt Mathilda's voice came over it, saying, "Mallory, are you there?"

Mallory reached over and pressed SPEAK. "Yes, I'm here," she said.

"Well, dear, I hate to have to tell you, but your cousin Skinny Norris just pulled in. He wants to ask you about fencing, and materials for a shed."

"O.K. I'm coming," Mallory said. Letting go of the button, she groaned.

"My mother told me he might stop by today," she said. "My uncle wants to repair a section of the fence around his house and build a new tool shed. I guess I'm going to have to see him."

"Not by yourself, you're not," Pete said emphatically. "It's bad enough that Skinny Norris is your cousin. You shouldn't also have to talk to him without some solid back-up."

"We've been dealing with him for years now – since long before you met him," Bob said. "We know how to really make him steam!"

"I don't want to make him steam," said Mallory rather gloomily. "I just want him to go away."

"We can do that, too," Pete said, leading the way out of Headquarters. As the four of them reached the edge of the outdoor workshop, the engine of Skinny's little red convertible sports car – originally parked right next to the Salvage Yard's Office – revved and the car lurched across the gravel and came to a screeching halt not far from where Pete and the others were standing.

To Pete's mind, this was far more dangerous and annoying than what Uncle Titus had done when *he* pulled into the Salvage Yard – especially because the driver of *this* car was grinning hideously beneath his porkpie cap.

As he unfolded himself from his car. his voice was gleeful. "Hello, frogs!" he said. "And, of course, my little cousin, Mally-Wally!"

"Frogs" was the term Skinny and some other upper-class students at Rocky Beach High used to refer to first-year students, but in some ways, it might have suited Skinny himself, Pete reflected. He was always amazed at how tall Skinny was, and how bony. He didn't look anything like Mallory, and yet today when Pete saw the two of them standing near one another, he *did* think there was something about them that was similar. Something about the shape of their ears.

However, that was as far as the resemblance went – and from what Mallory said next, it was clear she would have regretted having anyone notice that small and superficial detail.

"I've told you a hundred times not to call me Mally-Wally," she said. "So don't."

"As for frogs, we're sophomores now, so why don't you turn around and go find your other amphibious friends?" Bob said.

"Yes," Jupiter agreed. "All the toads, newts, and blindworms you hang out with."

Pete laughed aloud at this, but Skinny – full name E. Skinner Norris – just straightened up and looked around. He spotted the grindstone lying at the edge of the outdoor workshop and sneered.

"What's that, frogs?" he said. "Your new welcome mat?" He kicked some dust and gravel in its direction.

As he watched the dust fly, Pete once again found himself saying something he hadn't planned to. This happened more often

60

than he would have liked, and although it sometimes led to good results, it also sometimes didn't.

"Hey, watch it!" he said. "That's a memento of a case we haven't solved yet. A case in the Napa Valley – where there's a hotel called Castello Serreno that may have buried treasure."

Skinny stopped sneering and looked almost ominously interested – although he tried to cover his interest by saying, as he pointed to the grindstone, "It's cracked, just like the three of you."

"The four of us," said Bob. "Mallory is now a Special Consultant to our detective firm, and if we're cracked, she is, too."

To Pete, it looked as if Mallory would have preferred that Bob not tell Skinny about her new status – especially because Skinny immediately said, "Oh, yeah? Is her name on your precious card now?"

"Not yet," said Bob. "But I bet it will be. Though our business is none of yours. So tell us what you're doing here, or scram."

Skinny flashed a ghastly grin. "My father wants to fix our fence and build a tool shed, and he thought that among all the junk you have for sale, you might have something useful."

"Everything here is useful," Mallory said. "But only if you know how to use it. Do you have the design of the shed with you?"

"My father just told me to check out what you had for sale. I don't think he has a design yet," Skinny said.

"Luckily," Jupiter said, "we have two fine carpenters who could design whatever you want."

Skinny's eyes narrowed. "You mean like a special order?" he asked. "How much would that cost?"

"Since you're an old friend of ours, we could offer you a special deal," Jupiter said. "The regular rate plus twenty-five per cent."

Pete watched as Skinny tried to look superior to the persiflage but failed utterly. He pointed his long nose at the sky and sniffed.

"I told Dad this would never work," he said. "You call it salvage, I call it junk. See you around, frogs. And have fun *not* finding any treasure in the Napa Valley! At Castello Serreno or whatever the place is called!"

Before anyone could say anything more, he reinserted himself behind the wheel of his car, started the engine, and zoomed away.

"One more year," Mallory said, "and

then he'll be gone. At least I hope so. To college. If he gets in. Which is doubtful. Anyway, thanks for your moral support. He's such a git."

By now, Pete knew from Mallory that, in British slang, a git was a jerk, and Skinny was *certainly* that.

"Don't thank us," Bob said. "That was satisfying."

"Yes," Jupiter said. "I always enjoy conversing with Skinny. Just before he turns tail and runs."

"I don't," said Pete. "Not really. And I'm afraid I may have really put my foot in it when I mentioned Castello Serreno. You remember when Skinny got to Terror Castle even before we did?"

"What did he do when he got there?" asked Mallory.

"Not much but run away, as always," Jupiter told her.

"Even so, I wish I hadn't said it," Pete said ruefully.

"Don't worry about it," Bob said.

Just then Aunt Mathilda stuck her head out of the Salvage Yard's Office. "Why don't the four of you come down to the house? I'll make sandwiches. It's lunch time!"

Although this normally would have made Pete perfectly happy, his thoughts kept drifting back to his own careless comment – the one in which he'd told a human pest like Skinny Norris that Castello Serreno might have a hidden treasure. Why on earth had he said that? He could only hope it wouldn't lead to trouble down the road!

4

Mallory Changes Her Travel Plans

It was 1:30 the following afternoon, and while she waited for Worthington to pick her and the others up and take them to Phillipa Paxton's, Mallory was in her favorite shed, inventorying some of the stuff Uncle Titus had brought back from the Napa Valley the day before. Although she was usually quite focused when she took photographs and wrote descriptions of interesting salvage, today she'd found her mind wandering.

As she tried to find words to evoke a set of old mahogany spindles in such a way that they would sell quickly on the Salvage Yard website, she was thinking about too many things at once − her dreadful cousin Skinny, her upcoming trip to visit her father's cousin in Vancouver, Castello Serreno and The St. Francis Mountain Monastery − and, of course, Pete's suggestion that she design a new Three Investigators Headquarters.

Though Jupiter hadn't actually rejected Pete's suggestion, he hadn't approved it, either, and she didn't want to get her heart set on something that might not pan out in the end. Still, she couldn't help thinking that it would be a lot of fun to design a real building – or maybe take one of the Salvage Yard sheds and redesign it.

The shed she most liked to work in – the one she was in now – was quite close to the outdoor workshop, and if Jupiter *did* give her this assignment, then one way or another, she would want to leave the outdoor workshop where it was. She was also thinking that maybe the new Headquarters could have two entrances – one facing the side where the workshop would be, and one – smaller and more formal – facing the main gates.

But although Mallory really liked these ideas, she had no reason yet to think that Jupiter would want to go ahead, so she tried to put them out of her mind and think about calendar houses instead. She remembered as vividly as if it had been yesterday the trip she'd taken with her mother and father to the Orkney Islands, north of Scotland, where the three of them had taken a ferry ride from the island of Mainland to the island of Shapinsay.

From the deck of the ferry, she'd seen, rising from a field of blooming yellow flowers like something in a dream, a dark gray castle that wasn't a castle at all, but still had a wild assembly of turrets and chimneys and façades and roof lines.

Thinking of Balfour Castle made Mallory think about her father. Since she'd been looking forward to the first Three Investigators case of the summer, under other circumstances she might have been quite bummed out that she wouldn't be going to the Napa Valley the next day. But as it was, she wasn't.

Well, she was, in a way, of course, but she was also looking forward to finally meeting her father's first cousin Hamish − and secretly harboring hopes that he would be in some way like her father. Mallory's father Callum had been an engineer but also a natural leader − an extrovert who worked well with other people but did his most important work in the privacy of his own mind.

He'd been dead for eighteen months now, and although she still missed him every single day, Mallory was ready to find someone to start to take his place − and maybe his cousin would be that someone. Of course, when she thought of her own first cousin, Skinny, she knew that cousins could be very, very different − that her hopes might be dashed when she actually met this man about whom, at the moment, she knew very little.

Still, it was worth a shot, she reflected.

Just then, she heard footsteps outside the shed and Pete came pounding through the door.

"Worthington's here to take us to Phillipa Paxton's!" he said.

Mallory signed out on the time sheet, grabbed her backpack, and followed Pete toward the office where Worthington was climbing out of his Mini-Cooper.

He'd parked it right next to The Three Investigators' Ford Flex – a strangely handsome boxy car, painted in black and gray. Now he smiled and gallantly opened the passenger-side door for her. Mallory and Worthington had a special relationship – in part because both of them were originally from the U.K. – and Mallory tossed in her backpack, climbed into the front seat, thanked him, and fastened her seat belt.

In the back, Bob sat in the middle, with Jupiter on the right and Pete on the left, and in very short order they were on their way to Phillipa Paxton's. The one thing Mallory didn't like about the Flex was that it could be hard to hear the conversation in the back seat when you were sitting in the front, and today she had to strain to hear Bob and Jupiter talking about Phillipa Paxton.

Mallory had only met her twice before – at the boys' birthday party at the end of the previous summer, and when she, Pete, Bob and Jupiter had all gone to San Francisco for the opening of the John Frémont exhibition at the Museum of Material Culture – and in both cases there had been too many other people around for Mallory to get to know her even slightly.

As for Bob and Jupiter, they seemed to be wondering whether, this time, they'd meet her husband who'd been away, in London, the summer before.

Because Pete was sitting diagonally across from Mallory, she could hear him clearly. "Yeah," he said, "but even when we went to the Frémont exhibition, her husband *still* wasn't with her. I got the impression she might have been divorced."

By craning her neck a little, Mallory managed to hear Bob say, "And I bet you have a second husband picked out for her already, Pete! You think that just because you knew that Charlotte Mitchell and Connor O'Malley would like one another, you're a natural matchmaker!"

"Well, they *did* like one another, didn't they?" Pete said indignantly. "And even though Wally Tate and Isabella Chang are only roommates, they're also really happy, and they would never have gotten together if it hadn't been for The Three Investigators introducing them. Anyway, I was thinking that Hector Sebastian's supposed to be coming back from Wyoming for a month or two later this summer, and since Phillipa Paxton was *born* in Wyoming, and they both write books, maybe we should... "

Bob burst out laughing, and even Jupiter chuckled loudly enough for Mallory to hear. Since Mallory had never met Hector Sebastian and didn't know Phillipa Paxton at all well, she had no way of judging whether Pete's idea was a good one, but Bob and Jupiter were still amused as Worthington pulled up in front of Phillipa Paxton's house.

Through the Flex's window, Mallory saw, to her surprise, that it was southwestern in style. It had a red-tiled roof, white adobe walls, and dark-framed arched windows, and there was also a front porch supported by wooden poles. Everyone except for Worthington clambered out of the Flex and headed for a rustic-looking door made of thick weathered wood.

Jupiter knocked on the door with an old-fashioned door knocker.

Dr. Paxton came to open it, wearing a sleeveless cotton sun dress, and soon she had ushered the four of them into a very elegant, though comfortable, house. Inside, the walls were a pleasant white, hung with framed photographs and beautiful handmade rugs and tapestries. As Mallory looked around, it struck her that although *all* houses had been planned and designed by someone, it was only when they were elegant, or perfect, or in some way surprising, that you were able to see in them the outward manifestation of someone's idea. It was magical, really, the way a thought became a physical space.

She followed as Dr. Paxton led the way to a living room with a beehive fireplace in the corner and bookshelves everywhere else.

Dr. Paxton waited until they had gotten settled. "The last time I saw the four of you was in San Francisco, at the Museum of Material Culture," she said. "That was less than three months ago, but I'd swear you've all grown at least an inch!"

"Not me," said Bob, a bit glumly. "But Jupiter seems to be shooting up more every day."

"No one would ever know that people used to think he was stocky!" Pete said, nodding. "He's getting almost as tall as I am!"

That was true, Mallory realized suddenly. Although Pete had always been tall and powerfully built, over the course of the previous year, Jupiter had started catching up with him. Of course, he was leaner – less muscled than Pete – as befitted someone who had taken up fencing as enthusiastically and successfully as Jupiter had but who had never thrown a baseball or kicked a soccer ball in his life.

Also, his eyes were blue-green, instead of brown, and his hair was almost black, not brown like Pete's – but as she looked at him sitting in an easy chair near the beehive fireplace, Mallory thought that he was getting more good-looking all the time. This thought took her aback, and she was glad when Dr. Paxton picked up a file of papers and started to leaf through them.

"Before I tell you what I've discovered about Castello Serreno and the St. Francis Mountain Monastery, perhaps you'd be willing to tell me what brought them to your attention?" she asked.

"Of course," said Jupiter. "My Uncle Titus met the new owners of Castello Serreno on a recent buying trip to the Napa Valley, and they gave him an old broken grindstone with mysterious symbols on it. Later he learned that there were rumors that some sort of long-lost treasure was hidden in the building or on the grounds, and when we looked the building up online, we discovered its propinquity to the Mountain Monastery, and ...”

“What does propinquity mean?” Pete interrupted.

“Proximity,” said Jupiter. “Closeness, nearness. We also discovered that an astronomical observatory, which I assume was built at the Mountain Monastery in the late 19th century, has a stone set into the lintel above its entrance with a symbol identical to one of the symbols on the grindstone. I believe Bob brought a printout of the lintel.”

Bob unzipped the black portfolio in which he kept Three Investigators business, pulled out the printout, and handed it to Dr. Paxton. He also pulled out and unfolded the rubbing The Three Investigators and Mallory had done of the grindstone.

Dr. Paxton studied both of them closely. “That *is* interesting – though not entirely surprising, since I’ve discovered that the same man designed both the observatory and Castello Serreno. Like Giuseppi Donati – the man who commissioned the Victorian building – the architect was Italian, and he died very young, and in rather mysterious circumstances, apparently."

"Mysterious circumstances?" Jupiter asked intently.

"He vanished. Completely," Dr. Paxton said. "Since he wasn't yet married, and his parents lived in Pisa, Italy, there was no one to insist that the authorities investigate his disappearance properly. Although I haven't had time yet to do much research, I have the impression that the only people who cared very much were Giuseppi Donati and his wife. The architect, Alessandro Moretti, was apparently a second cousin – though considerably younger than Donati."

"Do you know anything else about him?" Bob asked.

"Not much," Phillipa Paxton said. "Just that he was a member of a Masonic lodge. Up until this morning, I didn't know much about Freemasons, but as it turns out, its main themes and symbols are geometrical and architectural. In fact, apparently in Freemasonry, the Supreme Being is referred to by the title of the Great Architect of the Universe or the

Grand Geometrician."

"Wow! That's really great," Bob said. "Really accurate, I mean. At least as a metaphor."

"Yes," Dr. Paxton agreed. "I'm guessing they chose to do that because people of all religions become Freemasons, and whoever founded the order didn't want to suggest that *his* God was the only God."

"Is God a big part of Freemasonry?" asked Pete.

"Yes," said Dr. Paxton. "In fact, belief in God is the primary requirement to become a Freemason; no atheist can be a member."

"When did Alessandro Moretti disappear?" asked Jupiter.

"In 1887 – just two or three months after what is now Castello Serreno was completed."

"Was Moretti Catholic, as well as a Freemason?" Jupiter asked.

"I assume so," said Dr. Paxton. "Almost all Italians were at that time, and the fact that he designed an astronomical observatory for an old Franciscan monastery suggests that he may have had a true devotion to Catholicism. The sad thing is that he seems to have been an excellent architect – almost an architectural engineer – but he only lived long enough to design five buildings. The three in San Francisco – his first three – all burned down in the Great Fire of 1905. His only remaining buildings are the two that you're interested in.

"I'd already decided that in *California Sunrise* – my new project – I'm only going to write about twenty or twenty-five buildings, and Alessandro Moretti's are going to be two of them. In fact, I'm planning to go up to Napa to see them for myself soon. Where are the four of you going to be staying when you go?"

Mallory noticed that she said "when you go," not "if you go," and as she realized that Dr. Paxton would also be heading to the Napa Valley, she felt a twinge of real regret that she herself *wasn't* going – at least not yet. Since she and her mother were flying to Vancouver through Sacramento, and Sacramento was only an hour or so from the southern part of the Napa Valley, maybe on the way back, she could leave the plane in Sacramento and join the boys.

As Jupiter explained to Dr. Paxton that Mallory wasn't actually coming with them, and that the boys had reservations to stay in the St. Francis Mountain Monastery, Mallory realized that even if she *did* get off the plane, she'd have no place to stay.

However, when Jupiter told Dr. Paxton that the Mountain Monastery didn't allow women in its guest quarters, Dr. Paxton surprised Mallory by saying, "If Mallory could come, after all, that really wouldn't matter; she and I could both stay in Castello Serreno. I called the place last evening, and Fortunata Serreno told me that although they still had a lot of work to do on the house, and they're not really open for business, they do have three guest rooms ready.

"She told me that when they're done they'll have fifteen guest rooms, as well as a library, a conservatory, a dining room, and lots of gardens for people to wander about in," Phillipa added. "Right now, there are just the three rooms, and one of them is already taken – by another historian, I gathered. Mrs. Serreno said he was writing a book on calendar houses."

Oh, no! thought Mallory. She'd really love to talk to a guy like that. In fact, the longer the conversation went on, the more unhappy she felt that she wasn't going to be able to go with The Three Investigators when they left for the Napa Valley. Still, if Phillipa Paxton was really inviting her to join her in one of the available rooms in Castello Serreno, she'd be crazy not to take her up on the invitation.

"Maybe I *could* come," she said, "if I can get off the plane in Sacramento, then get a ride to the Napa Valley."

"When I get there myself, I'll ask Mrs. Serreno if we can share my room if it turns out you *can* come," Phillipa Paxton said.

"That would be fantastic," said Mallory gratefully.

"I guess your husband won't be going with you, then?" asked Pete.

"We're not married any more," Dr. Paxton said. "Vincent spent so much time in Europe during the last year that we decided to call it quits – just before the Frémont Exhibition opened. The fact was, we'd grown apart – and we'd never had all that much in common to begin with, actually."

Both Jupiter and Bob looked at Pete, expressions of surprise and grudging admiration on their faces, but although Mallory could see that Pete was feeling proud at having called the situation correctly, she could also see that he didn't want to let Dr. Paxton see that.

"That's too bad," he said.

"Not really," said Dr. Paxton. "I feel freer than I've felt in years. Free enough to jump in the car tomorrow and drive to the Napa Valley without having to consult with anyone but Mrs. Serreno about it first. It'll be fun to be in on the beginning of a Three Investigators case – and maybe even help a bit. After all the help *you* gave *me*!"

"You've already helped us," said Jupiter. "Knowing that the architect of the Victorian castle was related to Giuseppi Donati would have been helpful all by itself, but the fact that Alessandro Moretti was also a Freemason – and that he disappeared the year the house was finished – may be truly significant leads. Do we have any friends or relatives who are Freemasons?" he asked, turning to the others.

They all shook their heads at this, but Pete said, "Maybe Worthington does! And anyway, how would we know whether we knew a Freemason or not? I thought it was some sort of secret society."

"I don't think members actually keep their *membership* secret," Bob said. "Not any more, at least. But since the only thing I really know about Freemasons is that they have a lot of secret passwords and handshakes and hand gestures, maybe at one time they actually did. Keep their membership secret."

"Did you discover anything else about

Giuseppi Donati or Alessandro Moretti?" asked Jupiter.

Dr. Paxton smiled, picked up the folder she had set back on the table, and plucked a paper from it – though instead of giving it to Jupiter, she kept holding it in her hand.

"I did, actually. The academic research site I was using to research Moretti had some cross-references that led me to a historian who's been studying 19th-century uses of a secret code or cipher in the western United States.

"It seems it's a simple geometric substitution cipher which exchanges symbols for letters, using a grid. I'm bad at pure abstractions, so what I read about the cipher seemed like Greek to me, but it may have originated with Hebrew rabbis and was supposedly also used by the Knights Templar during the Crusades."

"Who were the Knights Templar?" Pete asked curiously.

"A highly skilled unit of knights who wore white mantles decorated with a red cross when they went into battle," Jupiter replied.

To Mallory, it seemed that Jupiter's voice was suddenly filled with repressed interest, and as she looked at Bob and Pete, she saw that they, too, were getting more and more curious about the paper Dr. Paxton was holding in her hand.

"Union prisoners in Confederate camps also used the cipher to communicate during the Civil War," Dr. Paxton said. "Most famously, though, it was the cipher of choice for the Freemasons, who used it to keep their records of history and rites private, and for correspondence between lodge leaders. And guess what?" she asked, suddenly smiling.

"Well, what?" Pete asked excitedly.

"This historian who's been studying 19th-century uses of the cipher in the western United States found two letters written by Alessandro Moretti which used it. And guess what else? They were written to a man who seems to have been a Brother at the St. Francis Mountain Monastery during the years when the astronomical observatory was being built!

"That's all I know so far, but I printed out the name and contact information of the historian, and I thought that maybe Bob could ask him to e-mail a scan of the letters so that you can decode them," Phillipa concluded.

She handed the paper to Bob and glanced at her watch. "Well, I'd better start packing. I'm due at Castello Serreno tomorrow afternoon. I'll expect to see you up there after you've settled into your rooms at the monastery."

"With the new information you've given us, we may spend our first evening with the monks," Jupiter said. "Perhaps the monastery will have its own historian – or at least a librarian or archivist who may know something about the building of the astronomical observatory."

As everyone got to their feet to say goodbye, Mallory waited until the two of them were a little apart from the others.

"Could I really stay with you," she asked, "at Castello Serreno, if I can get to the Napa Valley?"

"Absolutely," said Dr. Paxton. "Just call me on my cellphone when you know if you can make it. Let me give you the number."

She walked into her office, pulled something off her desk, then came back and handed Mallory a card.

"This is totally brilliant," Mallory said. Then she followed Jupiter, Pete, and Bob to the car where Worthington was sitting reading a newspaper. She climbed into the passenger seat and yanked her seat belt down, then carefully tucked Dr. Paxton's card into a pants pocket.

While Worthington started up the car,

and Pete asked him if he'd ever known anyone who was a Freemason, Mallory started wondering how best to tell her mother about the coming change in her travel plans. It would be absolutely great, she reflected, to be able to stay in a calendar house a bit like the one in the Orkney Islands – but this time in the Napa Valley. What a fantastic way to start the summer!

5

Bob Solves A Puzzle

Bob didn't know why, but ever since he'd learned that Mallory wouldn't be coming with them to the Napa Valley – at least not at first – he'd felt a little less excited than he normally would have about the start of a new case. He and Jupiter were in the back seat of the Flex together, as usual, but since Mallory wasn't with them on the drive from Rocky Beach to the Napa Valley, Pete was sitting up front next to Worthington where he kept saying "Look at that!" as he pointed toward some new sight.

Bob normally loved Pete's enthusiasm, but after such a long drive he was ready for some quiet – or, at least, to get where they were going. Every time Pete said, "Look at that!" Bob jumped a little, jerked out of his thoughts about the case. While he knew that none of the inquiries he'd gotten had been all that exciting, at least they'd been sure things, and this current expedition wasn't. He hoped he didn't end up regretting persuading the team to pursue what might prove to be a wild goose chase.

The night before, Bob had e-mailed the historian whose name and contact information Phillipa Paxton had given him – after which he'd looked up the Freemason's cipher on the Internet and written down the code. Unfortunately, by the time he'd left Rocky Beach, Bob hadn't yet heard back from the historian, and now, after six hours in the Flex, he was wishing they weren't going to be staying in a place without any Wi-Fi.

Normally, Bob didn't mind not having a smartphone. He even understood why his parents (as well as Pete's parents and Jupiter's aunt and uncle) had decided that he and Pete and Jupiter shouldn't have fully Internet-connected cellphones until they were older. Being online every minute of every day and night was bad for the brain, and whatever research The Three Investigators needed to do could be done on his laptop.

But although that was generally true, Bob had recently started to think that (at the least!) it would be lighter and more convenient to carry a small portable device than a large one, and that there was a reason why smartphones had swept the world after they'd been invented. Luckily, his own mother and father had recently moved the date when he could get one back from the beginning of his junior year to the end of his sophomore one. In just one more year, he'd be able to access the Internet even in places which didn't have Wi-Fi.

Still, that didn't help him now. He was thinking of asking Worthington to stop at a fast food place or a gas station so that he could check his e-mail before they got to St. Francis Mountain Monastery when Worthington suddenly asked Pete whether he and the others had ever been to the Napa Valley before, and Pete was saying yes – though the last time he and Bob had come here, they'd flown.

"Also, Jupiter wasn't with us. Not at first," he told Worthington. "He had to take care of the Salvage Yard for Aunt Mathilda and Uncle Titus. Bob and I stayed with a woman named Lydia Green who owned a vineyard in Verdant Valley. She had a really cool nephew named Chang Green. He almost out-Jupitered Jupiter," Pete added, laughing. "He'd grown up in Hong Kong, and after the case, he went back there or we'd have seen him again, I'm sure!"

Worthington asked a few more questions about the old case, and as he remembered it, Bob felt a glow of something a lot like pride. As Mallory might say, he'd been chuffed by how well it had turned out, and since he and Pete and Chang Green had gotten along like a house afire, he wished he hadn't vanished completely out of The Three Investigators' life when he moved back to where he'd grown up.

It was too late to stop at a gas station, since Bob saw from the GPS he'd hung on the seat in front of him that they were already almost at the monastery. In fact, they were currently heading into the foothills, following a sign for St. Francis, and in very short order Worthington was pulling into a parking lot in front of a handsome stone building made of multicolored fieldstone.

To one side were two separate buildings. One was long and low, with smaller windows, while the other was square. Both were also made of fieldstone. Bob supposed that the bigger one was the monks' dormitory and that the square one was the monastery's guest house. It was quiet and beautiful. Worthington unstrapped their bicycles from the bike rack, and Jupiter and Pete unloaded their luggage from the roof rack as Bob looked down into the valley below him.

Somewhere in that valley – not more than five or six miles away – was the calendar house they'd come to see, and in the meantime they were doing something they'd never done before − staying in the guest house of a real, old-fashioned monastery.

In a nearby garden, Bob noticed a large and interesting-looking sundial, and from where he was standing, he could also look up into the hills and see the astronomical observatory perched on a hilltop. While Worthington and Pete stayed with the car, the bikes, and the luggage, Bob and Jupiter made their way to the main building, up a flight of stone steps to an arched wooden door over which hung a sign that read PEACE TO ALL WHO ENTER HERE.

Jupiter pushed open the heavy door and Bob found himself in a stone vestibule. A narrow hall stretched down the length of the building, and to their left, another door stood open. When Bob peered in, he saw a man with thick white hair wearing a brown cotton robe tied with a white rope belt. He was seated at a battered desk, studying a sheaf of papers.

Up until this moment, Bob had still been carrying a sort of grudge against the monastery for the fact that it wouldn't let girls or women sleep in its guest house, but there was something about actually being in a place that was mostly male, and entirely religious, that Bob suddenly found rather restful. It was weird, but also true.

He and Jupiter introduced themselves and greeted the monk, whose name was Brother Colin. They signed a guest book, and then Brother Colin gave them three cards which had the numbers of their guest rooms on them.

"We don't have keys here," he explained. "And you don't need to worry about anything being stolen. We've never had anything stolen from the guest house since it was opened. Your bikes will be safe if you just put them in the bike rack."

Bob was thinking that this sounded restful, too, when Jupiter startled him by saying, "In my own experience, you never know when a thief may show up. Thieves don't look any different from the rest of us. And surely you must keep the monastery's treasures under lock and key."

"Well, yes, we do," admitted Brother Colin. "Although Franciscan orders rarely have anything of much value in the way of gold or silver. The Jesuits who mostly settled California tended to have a lot of worldly treasures, but our biggest treasure is probably our archives. Only our abbot, Father John, and a few other monks have access to the key to the archive room. Though sometimes we have visiting scholars."

"How old do you have to be to be a visiting scholar?" Bob asked.

Brother Colin laughed. "No particular age that I know of. But Father John has to give personal permission, and this week he's in San Francisco attending to monastery business." Seeing the look of disappointment on Bob's face, he added, "He'll be back in a few days, though. If you want to see the archives, you can ask him then."

"Could I just send him an e-mail?" Bob asked – thinking that if he could get permission to do that, he could also check to see whether Phillipa Paxton's historian friend had written back and sent the coded letters.

"Father John doesn't use e-mail," Brother Colin said. "And neither do most of the brothers. In fact, our Wi-Fi is one thing we actually *do* lock up! Our Internet access is only available to monks who have dealings with the outside world. And it has a very clever password – one that is changed every day, on the stroke of midnight. Up until recently, the password was 'HelloBrother!', but a novice who recently joined us, and who has experience with computers, convinced us to make it harder to stumble on by accident.

"By the way, dinner is at 6:00," Brother Colin added. "In the refectory."

Brother Colin pulled out a map, showed them the location of the refectory and the three guest rooms, then marked them all with X's and handed Jupiter the map.

"I hope the three of you have a very restful and contemplative time here. If there's anything you need, just let me know," he said.

"We will. Thank you," said Jupiter. He glanced at the map, then turned toward the door. Bob followed him, and soon the two of them had rejoined Pete and Worthington. He was eager to start back to Rocky Beach but assured them he would come back to pick them up whenever they were ready to leave. They waved goodbye as he drove away, then found a bike rack on the side of the monastery.

"Should we lock the bikes up?" Pete asked.

"The monk we spoke with, Brother Colin, said that we wouldn't have to − that nothing had ever been stolen from either the guest rooms or the bike rack − so I don't think we should," Bob said. "Even if there *is* a thief about somewhere, it would look pretty rude after what Brother Colin told us."

"I agree," Jupiter said. "The monks are our hosts, and their wishes should be respected."

As they thrust their bikes into the bike rack, Pete asked, "Did Brother Colin say anything about dinner? Like what they serve and what time they serve it?" He looked hopeful.

Bob laughed. "The meal is at 6:00," he said. "But remember, the monks have taken a vow of poverty, chastity, and humility. We'll probably have bread and water."

He grinned, and Pete looked stricken until Jupiter and Bob both laughed.

Jupiter studied the map Brother Colin had given him and led the way to their rooms. They were basically identical – small and rectangular, tidy and spartan – and, to Bob, even more appealing in reality than they'd been in the photographs on the website.

A simple wooden cross hung over the bed, an old wooden desk and chair had been placed under the window, and a wooden wardrobe stood against the wall. A narrow single mattress was set on a wooden frame against the right-side wall – placed so that when Bob lay back with his head on the pillow, he was looking out the tall arched window.

He was startled when Pete stuck his head

in the door and said they both should go into Jupiter's room. There, Jupiter sat on the edge of his bed, pinching his bottom lip.

"What's up?" Bob asked him. "What are you thinking about?"

"The Wi-Fi password," Jupiter said. "It's a puzzle, after all, and I love puzzles. But I'm coming up blank. Every password reflects the mind of the person who created it, but we know absolutely nothing about the novice who came up with the new password. Not even his name. I'm hoping we'll meet him at dinner."

"So you can read his mind," Pete said.

"I don't need to read his mind," Jupiter said. "I just need to figure out how his mind works."

"So what should we do until dinner?" Pete asked.

"Let's go to the garden I saw earlier," said Bob. "You can see the observatory really well from there. If we have the time, we could even hike up to it."

Bob led the way. The sun had shifted, as had the shadows, so everything looked subtly different. The hike up to the observatory followed a path filled with switchbacks, so by the time they arrived, it was considerably later than they'd expected it would be. Bob stood for a while staring at the keystone at the top of the front door's arch – the stone with the symbol that matched the one on the grindstone that Uncle Titus had brought back – a triangle with a pointed base, and a "G" in the middle.

Jupiter examined it carefully, and then the three of them went inside and also examined the beautiful long telescope that was mounted on a housing, and that could be reached by climbing a few carved wooden steps. Bob found the observatory tranquil, but after climbing up and down the telescope housing's steps, Pete got a bit agitated – reminding them that dinner started at 6:00, and that they had better start down. Bob had always thought Pete had a clock in his stomach!

They found the refectory easily. Late afternoon sunlight streamed in through the western windows and the room was filled with monks all wearing brown cotton robes like the one Brother Colin had worn. The Three Investigators stood uncertainly until one of the monks welcomed them and showed them to a table seating six. He explained that the long table in the middle of the room was for the fully initiated monks, and that the smaller tables were for the novices and for guests staying in the guest house.

"It's our custom," the monk told them, "to recite a prayer together before dinner. You'll find a copy of tonight's prayer, with your name on it, resting on your place mat."

Just then, three youngish monks arrived and joined them at their table, but before they were all able to introduce themselves, an elderly monk got up from where he had been sitting at the main table, and all the monks in the room picked up their prayer sheets. Bob picked his up as well and stood in front of his chair, reciting along with the others.

Bob wasn't used to praying, but the experience of a room full of men reading in unison, expressing thanks for the food and asking for guidance and spiritual aid was strangely stirring. Then they all sat, making a big clatter as the chairs were pulled out, and a small group of monks carrying trays put platters of freshly baked bread and homemade cheeses, tomatoes and green beans and fried eggplant and sliced chicken on the tables.

The three novices sitting opposite Bob and his friends welcomed the boys to the monastery.

"Are you thinking of becoming monks, too?" one of them asked curiously. He was blond and fair-skinned, slender, with a narrow face and gray eyes. Bob noticed his fingernails had been bitten to the quick.

Pete seemed almost embarrassed by the question, but he answered, "Not really. I mean, not at all. But my family is Catholic."

The man smiled at him. "Mine wasn't," he said. "And when I was your age, I wouldn't have given a second thought to becoming a monk. By the way, I'm Brother Anders. Anders Bergmann," he said, as the boys also introduced themselves.

"Are you Scandinavian?" Bob asked. "We know two Norwegian carpenters who have the same blond hair and fair skin."

"You have a good eye," said Brother Anders. "But my father was Swedish, not Norwegian."

He introduced the monks on either side of him – Brother Anselm and Brother Gerald. When he turned his attention to Brother Anselm, Bob thought that he actually looked a little like Brother Anders – not as blond, and not as fair-skinned, but with the same narrow face.

As it turned out, Brothers Anselm and Gerald were in charge of the garden at the monastery – not the flower garden, but a vegetable garden Bob and the others hadn't seen yet. Brother Anselm said that the vegetable garden not only supplied the monastery's kitchen with fresh fruits and vegetables and herbs, but also produced enough excess produce so that they could sell it in local farmers' markets and to local hotels.

"Do you sell your goods online as well?" Jupiter asked.

"Not the vegetables or fruits," said Brother Anselm. "But we do sell honey from our skeps. That is to say, *we* don't. But the beekeeper does! Or rather, he asks one of the brothers who's permitted to use the Internet to do it. Like Brother Anders here."

"You use the Internet?" Jupiter asked – and when he did, Bob noticed that Jupiter was sounding suspiciously innocent as he asked his questions. Almost cherubically innocent, really. Bob smiled to himself as he tucked into his tomatoes and thought about how masterfully Jupiter could manage to seem a lot less intelligent than he actually was when he thought it would serve his needs.

Sure enough, when Brother Anders responded to Jupiter's question, it was in the tone you use when speaking to a slightly slow child.

"Well, some of us have to," he said. "And although I'm still only thirty, before I came to the monastery I had a whole other life.

I was a hedge fund manager, and in the course of my work, I got quite good at computers."

"Too good, perhaps," said Brother Anselm almost merrily. "But God moves in mysterious ways, and Brother Anders has been with us for four months now."

"And where were you before that?" asked Jupiter, as innocently as before.

This time it seemed to Bob that Jupiter's question was met with a certain embarrassment on the part of Brother Anders. In fact, when he answered, his voice was a little chilly – or maybe a little strained. It was almost as if he was trying to find a way to tell the truth without actually telling it.

"I lived in Sacramento," he said. "Though I was born in San Francisco. It was there that I made a success of my hedge fund."

"San Francisco is a wonderful city," said Jupiter as innocently as ever. "That bridge! That bay! What was your favorite part?"

Brother Anders seemed to relax a bit and responded somewhat condescendingly, "The whole city is glorious. A mix of order and chaos. The sort of order and chaos that all great cities have. Great churches nestled in dens of sin. Buried bodies next to buried treasure."

"Buried treasure?" Pete blurted out – and then fell silent, because (as Bob could feel) Jupiter had kicked him under the table. At the kick, Pete blushed a little and fell silent.

"What kind of buried treasure?" said Jupiter, making his face go slack. "I've heard there's a lot of pirate treasure scattered around the bay."

"Well, maybe," said Brother Anders. "But I wasn't speaking literally. I was just suggesting that human life is always a mix of the good and the bad, the dark and the light, the orderly and the disordered. Belief and disbelief. Faith and science."

Jupiter had finished his dinner and was pinching his lower lip. He seemed to be finished playing stupid for the time, so Bob said, "Speaking of science, before dinner we took a hike up to the observatory. It seems a lot newer than the monastery. Why did your forebears build an observatory to begin with? I've never heard of monks with telescopes."

"There was a monk here in the 1880s whose name was Brother Benedict," said Brother Anselm. "He was quite radical, really – a questioning sort of man. He believed that the Church had made terrible mistakes through the years. He thought the Inquisition was an abomination, and that its teaching that the earth and not the sun was at the center of the known universe needed to be atoned for."

"Yes," Brother Gerald said. "He wanted to teach the other brothers that since God could do anything, he could just as easily create a universe with the sun at its center as one with the earth at its center. The observatory would teach all brothers and guests and visitors the secrets and mysteries of God's creation."

Bob was quite interested in this new information. Brother Benedict must be the monk Alessandro Moretti had written to, using the Freemason's cipher. Once again, he was flooded with frustration that he couldn't check his e-mail to see if the historian had written back.

Still, all that he said was "You know that stone over the main door of the observatory? The one with the capital G? Do you know what that means?"

"No," Brother Gerald said. "I don't have any idea. But I'm sure that the architect who designed the observatory did. He left nothing to chance. Though in the end, chance seems to have won out. Not very long after he oversaw the completion of the observatory, he vanished. He was never heard from again."

Although he'd already heard this story, Bob almost shivered. He hated stories like that. They always had gruesome and unexpected endings.

Dinner had come to an end, and the monks who had served them were now clearing the tables. When Bob noticed that the monks all picked up the prayers with their names on it and took them away with them, he picked his up, too, and so did Pete and Jupiter.

Brother Anselm smiled and nodded at the gesture.

"We all keep our evening prayer sheets in our cells for an entire year. At the end of each year, we burn them. It's surprising how thick a sheaf of 365 prayer sheets – 366 during Leap Year! – can be. But just as each day is different, so, too, is each prayer, and keeping our prayers for an entire cycle around the sun reminds us of the order of God's great universe."

"Wow! I like that a lot!" Pete said.

"We must let the other novices get their work done," Brother Gerald interjected kindly. "It was a pleasure meeting all of you. We all get up pretty early, so we may not see you at breakfast, but we'll see you at dinner tomorrow night."

The boys all nodded, and as they walked back to the guest house carrying their prayers, Bob could see that Jupiter was still pinching his bottom lip.

"Jupe," he said, "what is it?"

"I'm sorry I kicked you, Pete," Jupiter said.

"That's O.K.," said Pete. "It didn't really hurt. I guess you didn't want me to mention the rumors about Castello Serreno, huh?"

"That's right," Jupiter said. "I didn't. Although I have no reason to think that this monastery and its inhabitants aren't exactly what they seem, I saw no reason to let the monks know more about us than they need to. At the moment, they don't know that we're investigators, and I want to keep it that way."

When they got to their rooms, Jupiter added, "Since it seems obvious that the man Brother Colin referred to − the novice who created a new password for the monastery − is Brother Anders, and since he gave us quite a lot of information about his background when we talked to him, why don't we go into Bob's room and see if we can figure out the password for the monastery's Wi-Fi?"

Soon, they were all sitting together on the edge of Bob's bed − where Bob accessed

the monastery's secure Wi-Fi network, then
stared at the box that asked him to enter the
password.

"The thing is," he explained to Pete,
"Brother Colin told us that the password is
changed every night at midnight, so whatever it
may be today, it will be different tomorrow.
That makes it pretty hard to crack."

"Try Alessandro Moretti first," Jupiter
said. "All in one word. When Brother Gerald
was talking about the man who'd designed the
observatory, it seemed to me that Brother Anders was looking very interested. Interested in a
peculiar way."

Bob typed in the name and pressed En-
ter. It didn't surprise him when it was rejected.

"That's not it," he said. "And I really
don't see why it would be."

"How about order and chaos?" Jupiter
asked.

"Or buried treasures, or buried bodies?"
Pete said.

After trying all of these ideas in multiple
combinations, Bob said, "We're never going to
get it. We could try for 365 days straight, and
it still wouldn't happen. And anyway, I'm not
sure we even ought to do this. I mean, Brother
Colin   seemed   to   think   it   was   a   form   of

stealing."

"It's in service to a noble calling," Jupiter said. "We're not using the Internet mindlessly. We're investigating!"

"That's true," said Bob, and as he sat there wondering how on earth you could deduce a password which changed every day, he happened to glance at the prayer sheets he and Pete and Jupiter had brought back from the refectory. As he thought about Brother Gerald saying that the monks all kept their evening prayer sheets in their cells for an entire year, he suddenly wondered if maybe the daily password was the first word of the daily prayer. Without sharing this thought with his friends yet, Bob grabbed his prayer sheet, glanced at it, and typed "Godofourfathers" in the box for the password. Then he hit ENTER.

And he was online! "We're in!" he yelled. He suddenly felt completely happy. And when he checked the firm's e-mail and found that not only had the historian written back to him – attaching JPGS of the letters he'd discovered – but that Phillipa Paxton had sent a note to say she'd checked into her room at Castello Serreno, Bob suddenly felt totally confident that this case really would lead to something.

He felt it even more strongly when Jupiter asked him to explain the thought process by which he'd arrived at his sudden insight. When he had, Jupiter said, "Well done, Bob. A truly impressive piece of deduction." Praise from Jupiter always felt really good!

6

Some Very Exciting Letters

Ten minutes later, Jupiter, Bob, and Pete were all staring down at the scans of Alessandro Moretti's letters on Bob's laptop. Although Pete was still talking about Bob's amazing insight, Jupiter was now focused on the cipher symbols – which looked a bit like hieroglyphs when taken all together.

Individually, Jupiter realized, they resembled right angles, or the three sides of a rectangle, or the tip of an arrow – some with dots in them and some without, all of them evenly spaced and running from line to line in an uninterrupted fashion. He felt a tingly jolt of pleasure. Even though the letter made no sense at the moment, he knew it would soon give up its secrets, and he also felt that way about the case as a whole.

"Boy," Pete said, "that sure looks weird."

"Yes," Jupiter said. "Its appearance makes it look a good bit more daunting than it is, though. Of course, when you know a cipher's code, it always looks easy. I can't imagine what this must have looked like to people who had no idea how to decipher it."

"Remember when we first heard pig Latin?" Bob said. "It sounded incomprehensible. But it's actually easy."

"Iyay ememberray," Pete said.

"Osay oday Iyay," Jupiter said.

"I was reading up on the Freemason's cipher last night," Bob said. "It's also called the pigpen cipher."

"Eyeway isyay ityay alledcay atthay?" Pete asked.

"Enough!" Jupiter said, wincing. "But it's a good question."

Bob pointed to several of the symbols in Moretti's letter – ones that looked like three sides of a square with a dot in the middle.

"Some smart aleck thought the lines looked like a pen. And the dot is the pig!" Bob said.

Everybody laughed. Jupiter found that despite his own lack of insight about the password, he was in an excellent mood. He'd enjoyed dinner and meeting the monks, but he'd enjoyed even more being able to praise Bob for what he'd deduced. Ever since they'd left Rocky Beach, he'd sensed that Bob was feeling down, and now, with his password triumph, he no longer was.

"How are we going to decode the letters?" Pete asked.

"Slowly, and by hand," Jupiter said. "We don't have a printer, so we'll have to work from the JPGS on Bob's laptop. Bob, could you find a copy of the cipher itself and copy it down so we'll know what we're doing?"

He watched as Bob quickly found the code for the pigpen cipher online and then copied it with a black marker onto a sheet of paper. Jupiter had seen the cipher before, but he was still intrigued by its simplicity.

It consisted of two grids, like the ones used in tic-tac-toe, and two large Xs. The first grid contained the beginning letters of the alphabet, in order, starting at the upper left with A and ending in the bottom right with I. The second grid started with J and ended with R. But the nine squares of the second grid all contained a dot as well, to differentiate them from the first grid.

Then the two large Xs. In the four Vs that the first X formed, S was at the top, V was at the bottom, and T and U were to the left and right, an unorthodox arrangement. In the second X, the same pattern was used, with W and Z at the top and bottom and X and Y to the left and right. And in the same way that the second grid was different from the first, the second X was different in that there were dots in the crux where the two intersecting lines of the X came together.

It would be easy to remember, Jupiter thought, so long as you didn't make a mistake with the arrangement of letters in the two Xs.

Jupiter studied the opening of the first letter. The symbols ran uninterruptedly from margin to margin and lacked all the things that readers were used to and depended on – spaces and punctuation.

"That is a long line of I-don't-know-what-it-means," he said. "Let's take it one symbol at a time." He looked back and forth between the JPG of the letter on Bob's laptop and the cipher Bob had copied. "The first symbol is a J," he said. "Then an A, then an N."

Bob carefully wrote down the letters as Jupiter uttered them. "That could be the beginning of 'January,'" he said. "Most letters start with the date the letter is being written. Maybe Moretti spelled out the numbers because they're not in the code."

"Good thinking, Bob," Jupiter said. He kept transcribing, and in short order, Bob had written "januaryfouroneeightninezero."

"It's all run together," Pete said.

"Yes," Bob said. "When all the letters are transcribed, we'll have to separate the words and add the punctuation. Let's keep going."

dearbrotherbenedict came next.

"Wow!" Pete said after the beginning of the letter had been deciphered. "Brother Benedict and a bunch of the monks caught the Russian flu. I've never even heard of it."

"Neither have I," Jupiter said, "though it sounds pretty serious if the monastery was put under quarantine. Bob, see what you can find out."

Jupiter watched as Bob opened another tab in his browser and searched for "Russian flu." As he read aloud the article he found, Jupiter was amazed. He had, of course, heard of the flu pandemic of 1918-1920, which had killed as many as fifty million people worldwide. But shouldn't he have also heard of the Russian flu of 1889-90 – even if it had only killed a million? A million was still a very large number, he thought.

The pandemic had started in St. Petersburg, Russia, and infected half the city's population before spreading across Europe – where it had sickened everyone from ordinary people to heads of state like the king of Belgium and the emperor of the Austro-Hungarian empire.

Jupiter was fascinated to learn how people tracking the flu's spread were able to demonstrate for the first time that human beings were giving it to one another. Earlier theories suggested that diseases were spread on the wind, but the transmission of the Russian flu clearly followed the routes that people took when traveling – rivers, roads, and the relatively new railway lines.

The disease crossed the Atlantic on steamships, where it landed in New York and Boston, and then spread across the country to the west coast on the country's railroads. It was the sort of rabbit hole Jupiter knew could distract them for much of the evening, so he pulled them back to the task at hand.

"So Brother Benedict was sick, and Alessandro Moretti couldn't visit him," he said. "That's why he wrote the letters. Back to work!" he said.

He, Pete, and Bob kept at it until all the symbols in the first letter had been decoded. Then Bob went through it carefully, cleaning it up, adding capital letters, dividing the deciphered code first into words and then into paragraphs, and adding punctuation. After that, they were a great deal easier to read.

The first letter read:

January Four, One Thousand Eight Hundred Ninety.

Dear Brother Benedict,

I was sorry to hear that you and others in your order have been stricken with the Russian flu, and that no visits to the monastery are currently allowed, but I am pleased to confirm that the items in which you and I both have such an ardent interest will soon have a hidden home in a public house I am designing.

None would guess from my blueprints that so many instruments which were ultimately designed by the Great Architect of the Universe will, in the not-too-distant future, be folded into a cloak of darkness — a cloak of darkness which can be folded back to let the light from the sun in.

If your health permits it, please let me know that you have received and decoded this letter. When I hear back, I will give you further details.

In the meanwhile, I hope that the sundial I designed for the monastery's front garden is giving proper information.

"The items will soon have a hidden home!" Pete crowed. "That's proof of the hidden treasure. It's not a rumor. It's a fact!"

"It would seem so," Jupiter said.

"But Moretti is being super vague," Bob said. "What do you think he means by a cloak of darkness that can be folded back?"

"I don't know," Jupiter said. "Fabric can be folded, but surely not darkness."

"What could the 'items' be?" Bob wondered.

"Jewels?" Pete asked.

"Why would a monk who had taken a vow of poverty have an ardent interest in jewels?" Jupiter asked. "No, I think it's something else. Besides, later in the letter he calls the items 'instruments'"

"Like musical instruments?" Bob asked.

"Why would *they* be valuable?" Pete asked.

"Maybe because they're very old, or made by someone famous. You've heard of Stradivarius violins," Bob asked.

"Not really," said Pete.

"What other types of instruments are there?" Jupiter mused. "Medical instruments? Meteorological instruments? Mathematical instruments?" He looked at Pete and saw that his questions were dampening his friend's enthusiasm. "But we also learned that Moretti designed that sundial we saw in the garden earlier. Let's go look at it again before it gets dark."

"Sure," Bob said. "But shouldn't we transcribe the second letter?"

They got back to work. This time, the transcription went more quickly. The second letter read:

January Twenty, One Thousand Eight Hundred and Ninety

Dear Brother Benedict,

I was pleased to learn that my previous communication reached you in a timely manner, and that you were able to make sense of it.

Please accept my sympathy on the distress you have been experiencing, and my congratulations that you seem to be on the mend. I will look forward to seeing you again in person when I travel to St. Francis for the opening of the observatory.

By then, I expect to be able to give you full details as to the housing I have devised for the Grand Geometrician's treasured instruments. I think you will approve of it. For now, suffice to say that the number 12 has proven quite important, as has the number 7, but that the most important thing of all is that light shall illuminate the darkness!

With Kindest Regards,

Alessandro Monetti

"These two guys knew one another," Pete said. "Right?"

"Correct," Jupiter said. "It sounds from the tone of the two letters that they were good friends."

"So why is Moretti taking all the time and trouble to use this pigpen stuff?" Pete asked.

"Well," Jupiter said. He had to admit it was a good question, and one he hadn't thought of. The fact was, he hadn't yet quite recovered from the odd way this case had started – with his uncle asking him that puzzle about the wine cask, and then telling him and the others that he was giving them a memento of a case they hadn't solved yet. Why *wasn't* Moretti just writing his letters in regular English? It wasn't as though he was giving information that anyone could use; all his language was poetic and meant to conceal rather than reveal.

"I'm not really certain," he said. "Though the letters were written in the first place because the monastery was under quarantine – and it would seem that both Moretti and Brother Benedict were Freemasons."

"Maybe Moretti was just having fun," Bob said. "It's all very cloak-and-dagger."

"It's all very cloak of darkness," Pete said. "And more instruments! The Grand Geometrician's treasured instruments. Who's the Grand Geometrician anyway?"

"Didn't Phillipa Paxton say it refers to God?" Bob said, "Though in the first letter Moretti calls him the Great Architect. Now that I think of it," Bob added, "can a monk be a Freemason?"

"I don't see why not," Jupiter said. "The one prerequisite to join the Freemasons is a belief in God, and monks would surely qualify."

"Would a monk leave the monastery and attend meetings with other Masons?" Bob asked.

"Perhaps Brother Benedict was a Mason before he became a monk," Jupiter said. "But right now, I don't know, and since it's not getting any earlier, and I want to look at that sundial before the sun goes down, maybe we should do that now."

"I looked at it when we first got here," Bob said. "It didn't seem like anything special or unusual."

"Even so," said Jupiter, "I think we should look again now that we know that Moretti designed it."

Bob put his laptop away and Jupiter tidied the papers they'd been working with. Then, after grabbing a small flashlight in case it got too dark, he led them out of the guest house. As they left, he was surprised to see a boy who looked to be in his late teens raking the lawn. He had blondish hair, in a crewcut, and an open friendly face.

Pete, always the most outgoing of the three of them, went right up to him. "Hi," he said. "It's pretty late in the day to be working, isn't it?"

The boy leaned on his rake and stared at Pete, Jupiter, and Bob. He seemed surprised to see others not much younger than himself on the monastery grounds until it dawned on him.

"You must be staying in the guest house," he said.

"You got it," Pete said. "We're from southern California." He introduced Jupiter and Bob and then himself.

"I'm Chauncey Kit," the boy said, shaking their hands. "I should be home by now, but my ride never showed up so I had to take my bike. That's why I'm working so late. Actually I ride my bike up here a lot. It's a good workout."

"So you live close to here?" Jupiter asked.

"Not that far," Chauncey said. "Maybe seven or eight miles. My folks own a small campground in the valley. Actually it's more for small RVs than for tenters. We have showers and water hookups and stuff like that. Most of our visitors come to see the vineyards and stay for a few days, but you guys seem too young for that."

"Actually," Jupiter said. "We're here to visit Castello Serreno, but it's not taking guests at the moment. So we're staying here."

Chauncey nodded as though that made perfect sense. "I haven't met the Serrenos yet," Chauncey said. "My folks say they're good people."

"You've been there?" Bob asked. "Before the Serrenos bought it?"

"Sure," Chauncey said. "I knew the Beauchamps pretty well. I did some yard and garden work for them too."

"Great!" Pete said. "Maybe you can help us. Have you ever heard the story about the hidden treasure on the property?"

Chauncey laughed. "I hope that's not what you're here for," he said. "Because that's all it is – a story. Everyone in the valley's heard it, so I can promise you that if there was any treasure, it would have been found long ago. The Beauchamps joked about it from time to time. They never really believed it."

Chauncey took a few more tentative swipes with his rake and then picked up what he'd gathered and put it in a wheelbarrow. "Where did you say you guys are from?"

"It's a small town north of L.A.," Jupiter told him. "Rocky Beach."

"Are you treasure hunters?" Chauncey asked.

"Actually, we're truth hunters," Jupiter told him. "We're up here mainly because we're interested in calendar houses and we just found out that the building the Serrenos bought is a calendar house."

"Yep," Chauncey said. "Darndest thing. I mean, who would build a house worrying about the number of rooms or doors or panes of glass?"

"It is an odd idea," Jupiter said. "But it has a certain beauty to it." As an idea, he actually liked it a lot more than he was admitting at the moment. He also thought that it fit in perfectly with the Freemason's idea of God as the Great Architect or the Grand Geometrician. You didn't often find physical structures that expressed an interest in the poetry of science. And yet it *did* have a kind of poetry about it, Jupiter thought.

"Come to think of it," Chauncey said. "There was one time I was there, working in the big perennial border, and the Beauchamps' kids got all excited about the treasure thing. They spent the whole morning counting the panes of glass in the house, thinking it might lead somewhere. But they were disappointed to find it wasn't true."

"What wasn't true?" Jupiter asked, quite intently.

"Everyone always thought there were 365 panes of glass. Like for the days of the year? But the kids found out there were only

353. It sort of let the air out of everyone's balloon."

"Well," Jupiter said. "From what we understand, the house was built a long time ago, almost a hundred and fifty years. Maybe some of the windows have been replaced or redesigned or reconfigured since then. Even so, that *is* very interesting. That twelve panes of glass seem to be missing from the house."

It was very interesting, too – but since the day was growing ever more dim around them, he said, "It's been a pleasure meeting you, Chauncey, and I'm sorry to cut this short. But we've heard there's a sundial in the garden here, and we wanted to see it before it gets too dark."

"It *is* getting dark!" Chauncey said. "And I have to be getting home, anyway. By the way, if you're going to the calendar house, be sure to check out the garden there. It has seven sundials – including one that looks exactly like the one in the monastery garden."

Jupiter was starting to get the tingly feeling he got when a case was really underway. Of course he knew that Alessandro Moretti had designed both the calendar house and the monastery sundial, but until now he'd heard nothing about a garden with seven sundials at

Castello Serreno. Seven seemed excessive, which meant it wasn't something that had happened by chance, which meant that it meant something – something he'd have to figure out in the course of solving the case.

But as excited as he suddenly was, he didn't want to appear that way to Chauncey – or even, at the moment, to Pete and Bob. Chauncey was about to wheel away the garden debris when Jupiter said, "We'll only be here a few days, but maybe we'll see you again."

"I hope so," Chauncey said, grinning.

As Bob led the way across the lawn to the garden, Jupiter found he was pinching his lower lip. Why had Moretti designed seven sundials? Just to mirror the seven days of the week? But if he was precise in that regard, why would the calendar house have only 353 panes of glass? Had the Beauchamp children been mistaken? Or were twelve panes of glass really missing? Suddenly, Jupiter couldn't wait to see the house and maybe even count the panes of glass for himself.

The sun had set by the time they reached the sundial in the garden, and twilight was upon them. The sundial's central brass plate had lost much of its luster, but the thing itself was of a kind that Jupiter was familiar with.

The brass plate was set horizontally, in line with the earth's surface, and fastened to a foot-high marble pedestal.

The sundial's face had been inscribed like the face of a clock but with the numbers spaced irregularly, closer at the bottom, where 5, 6, 7, and 8 bunched together. Jupiter knew the adjustment had been made according to the latitude at which the sundial was placed, taking into account the angle at which the rays of the sun hit the earth.

On the sundial's face a vertical triangular blade had been placed. It was this that cast the shadow that told the time. Jupiter knew it was called a gnomon. In fact, an earlier case, in which he, Bob, and Pete had recovered a spectacular ruby called the Fiery Eye had been solved when the peak of a mountain had acted as a gnomon for a gigantic sundial.

"Bob was right," Pete said. "It's just a regular sundial, not like the one in Dial Canyon."

"I didn't check when I was here earlier to see if worked," Bob said.

"It looks like it ought to work," Jupiter said. "From everything we know about Alessandro Moretti, he was a serious man who designed things with a purpose in mind. Nothing frivolous about him."

"Except for writing letters in cipher just for the fun of it," Bob said. "If that's what he did."

"You brought a flashlight, didn't you?" Pete asked. "Would a sundial work with a flashlight?"

"No," Jupiter said. "Not unless I could jump up into the sky and approximate the angle of the sun's rays."

"Better not try it," Pete said.

Nevertheless, Jupiter took his flashlight out of his pocket and turned it on.

"Let me borrow that," Pete said, grabbing it out of Jupiter's hand. He placed its light under his chin, casting strange and spooky shafts of light and shadow upward over his face, as the three of them had done when they were younger. But Jupiter wasn't into playing at the moment.

He took the flashlight back and shone it on the sundial's metal face. Suddenly, he saw something inscribed on the brass that he hadn't seen before. It was fainter than the numbers of the hours and the lines that radiated from the plate's center. It was written across the lower half of the sundial in flowery script.

"Look at that," he said.

Pete and Bob clustered around him and stared at the spot where he was focusing the flashlight's beam.

"Wow!" Pete said. And then he read the words aloud slowly.

"*Eppur si muove*," he read.

"Not English," Bob said, stating the obvious.

Pete's interest seemed to be suddenly piqued.

"That word there," he said, pointing with his finger at *muove*. It's a lot like the Spanish verb *mover* − to move. *Muevo, mueves, mueve.* I move, you move, it moves. I bet it's Italian."

Jupiter was flooded with excitement. Of course it was Italian! he thought.

"You're right, Pete," he said, "on both counts. I'm not a betting man but I would bet a very great deal that that's the Italian of Galileo's famous words 'And yet it moves'!"

"Yikes!" Pete said.

"I'm sure you're right, Jupe," Bob said.

Jupiter held the flashlight under his chin, like Pete had, throwing shafts of light up over his face. He made mysterious ululations with his voice. He was filled with elation.

Pete and Bob both laughed.

"Scary!" Pete said.

Then Jupiter turned off the flashlight and stood in the darkness with his two best friends. Overhead, the sky was sprinkled with the evening's first stars – glorious stars, an astronomer's treasure.

"Come on," Jupiter said, after they'd stood for a few minutes in silence, looking up. "We'd better get back to our cells."

He had a feeling that tomorrow, and their first visit to Castello Serreno, was going to be both stimulating and enlightening. And maybe more than that.

Around them, the roses and lilies had taken on shades of blue and gray in the gathering darkness. But the air smelled sweet, and the twining vines on the trellises sent their tendrils toward the stars that were punching through the deep blue fabric of the sky, like tiny silver studs – and somehow all this made Jupiter feel certain that what lay ahead was going to be a complex, satisfying, exciting case.

7

Castello Serreno

Pete didn't know what Jupiter was thinking, of course, but if he had, he would have wondered why it had taken him so long to arrive at the same conclusion Pete had arrived at the moment he heard the rumors of hidden treasure. The next morning, when he and his friends got on their bikes to head for Castello Serreno, he was in a tearing hurry to get there, but when he reached the hotel sign at the end of the long gravel driveway, he waited for Jupiter and Bob to catch up.

After that, the three of them rode abreast. The further they went, the bigger and more impressive the building at the end of the driveway became. Pete had seen plenty of Victorian houses, especially in San Francisco, but the ones he'd seen there had been mostly tall, narrow, and deep. This one was wide and long and very, very big.

The house was painted in warm, bright colors. A row of tall windows rose on either side of a massive front door, which was flanked by leaded glass sidelights and topped with a

127

glass transom. At each of the house's four cor-
ners were round towers with tops like witch's
caps, while the front of the house had a porch
running for its entire length – and there was
Phillipa Paxton on the front porch waiting for
them!

She was wearing a simple shift and a big
straw hat, and when she saw them, she jumped
to her feet and waved.

They all jumped off their bikes, and once
they had parked them, ran up the wooden
steps. "Hello, Dr. Paxton!" Pete said.

"Good Lord, Pete," Phillipa Paxton said.
"I think we're old enough friends so that you
can call me by my first name!"

"O.K.," Pete said, blushing. When Jupiter and Bob had clattered up the steps and
joined them, Phillipa urged them all to sit with
her in a semicircle of rocking chairs.

"We made it!" she said. "Felix and Fortunata have gone to town to do some shop-
ping, but they'll be back soon. Such lovely people! How's the monastery?"

"It's great!" Bob said. "Very quiet. Excellent for sleeping."

"Good," Phillipa said, "since that's what
you'll mostly do there. Actually I'm glad to have
this time alone with you so I can catch you up

on everything. I just got here yesterday, but there's quite a lot to tell."

"Have you met the other guest yet?" Jupiter asked.

"Just barely," Phillipa said. "He told me he's writing a book about calendar houses and plans to feature this hotel. I haven't talked to him much, but I hope to find out more about him at lunch today. You'll meet him then."

"What are Mr. and Mrs. Serreno like?" Pete asked.

"I think they're going to make a big success of this place," Phillipa said. "They're perfect hosts, just the sort of people who ought to run a small hotel. They made me feel welcome right away – and as though I'd known them forever. They were both born in Lisbon, Portugal and come from Muslim families."

"Muslim?" Pete asked, surprised. "I thought Muslims came from the Middle East."

"Felix's ancestors came from Tunisia," Phillipa said, "and Fortunata's from Egypt – though I didn't get the impression that either of them is particularly religious. Last night at dinner, we got to talking and they said that neither of them knew as much about their family histories as they would like." She laughed. "They thought my having grown up in Wyoming was far more exotic than either of their stories. They wanted to know all about cow pokes and 'git along, little dogies'."

Although Pete was having trouble suppressing his impulse to start running around Castello Serreno looking for the hidden treasure, he listened as Phillipa filled them in on what she had learned.

Apparently, Felix Serreno's family had owned a small hotel in Lisbon, and ever since he'd been very young, it was assumed he'd follow in the family tradition. Felix had told Phillipa that his first love was the study of history, but he didn't see any way he could make a living from it. So after he and Fortunata were married in Lisbon, they had come to the United States to study at the Cornell School of Hotel Management in upstate New York.

"They did so well that they were offered jobs all over the country, and they chose to move to San Francisco where they ran a small boutique hotel that had just opened," Phillipa said. "It was a huge success and they made very good money. The name Fortunata means fortunate, and Felix means lucky."

"Wow," Pete said. "It sounds like they were given the right names!"

Phillipa laughed. "Yes, indeed," she said.

"But that's only part of it. They're also incredibly nice and both of them are very hard workers. While they were in San Francisco, they became United States citizens and had their first child. Fortunata is pregnant again – and, of course, they took all the money they'd made and bought this house."

"That's certainly an American success story," Jupiter said.

"Yes, it is," Phillipa said. "Though I'm sure they'd have done just as well if they'd stayed in Portugal. What about the three of you? What have *you* been up to?"

"That historian you found who's studying the Freemason cipher?" Bob said. "I e-mailed him, and he wrote back. He sent the two Moretti letters and we decoded them last night."

Phillipa Paxton's face was alive with interest.

"They mentioned the treasure," Pete said. "'Folded into a cloak of darkness'."

"Really!" Phillipa Paxton said. "He used those words? That's certainly mysterious."

"Yes," Jupiter said. Pete could see he was trying to hide his excitement from Phillipa. "We have no idea what that means. Yet."

Just then a car came up the gravel drive

and all four of them stopped talking and watched it come closer and then park next to the other cars in front of the building. The Serrenos! Pete thought. The boys jumped to their feet.

Fortunata Serreno was about six months pregnant and she held a toddler by the hand. She was young and merry-looking. Her white blouse contrasted sharply with a long dark loose-fitting skirt that reached almost to the ground. Over her shoulders, she wore a nice silk scarf, brown and green and gold, knotted on her chest.

The child, a young boy with long curly hair and a mischievous smile, looked up at his mother and put his fingers in his mouth.

"You must be The Three Investigators," she said. "But you are all so young!" She turned and called to her husband who was retrieving some brown paper bags from the trunk of the car. "Felix? The boys are here!"

Felix Serreno was tall and slender, with very short black hair. His skin was slightly dark, like that of the woman and child. He had a closely cropped beard and mustache and wore round gold-rimmed glasses. His face was earnest, friendly, open. He looked more like a scholar than a hotelkeeper, Pete thought.

"Welcome!" he said. "You will forgive me for not shaking your hands. Mine, as you can see, are occupied." He smiled winningly and then bowed slightly from the waist. "I am Feliciano Serreno, though everyone calls me Felix. You have met Fortunata. And this little one is Luciano. Light of the day. We have been many times blessed."

"Will you call him Lucky?" Jupiter asked.

Felix Serreno smiled. "You are very clever, but no. We do not wish to tempt fate."

Jupiter said, "I'm Jupiter Jones, and these are my friends and partners Pete Crenshaw and Bob Andrews." Pete smiled as Jupe reached into his pocket, drew forth one of their business cards, and offered it to Felix Serreno. He put the bags he was carrying down on a wooden side table and examined the card. In Pete's opinion, that meant the chase was officially on!

"I don't know how much Dr. Paxton has told you about us, but the reason we're here is because you recently sold an old grindstone to my uncle Titus Jones – " Jupiter started to say.

"Yes!" Felix said. "Just last week! A delightful man."

"And he told us the rumors about hidden treasure on the property. He also said he mentioned us to you," Jupiter finished.

"Indeed!" Felix Serreno said. "I told him I wished you were here to solve the mystery. And now here you are!"

Fortunata had let go of her son, and Luciano stumbled over and grabbed onto Pete's leg. Pete stooped down, picked the boy up, and bounced him up and down. Luciano shouted with joy.

"I see you have a way with children," Fortunata said. "That is a gift."

"Thanks," Pete said. "But sometimes I think it's because I'm still a kid myself."

Everybody laughed, which made Luciano shout again.

"You can give him back to me if you want," Fortunata said.

"No," Pete said. "I'm good." He smiled at the boy who smiled back.

"Did you know that the grindstone Jupiter's uncle gave us had been engraved?" Bob asked Felix Serreno. "Our friend Mallory showed us how to rub it with a sheet of paper and a piece of charcoal and we found the name of Galileo and the dates of his birth and death, as well as the four moons of Jupiter that he discovered in 1610."

Felix looked astonished. "Really?" he

said. "I wish I had known that. I might not have been so ready to sell it to your uncle. I have always been interested in astronomy. When you get a chance to explore the house, you will be amazed to find that there are beautiful wood carvings related to astronomy in many rooms – carvings of astrolabes in particular. Do you know what an astrolabe is?"

Pete glanced at Bob and Jupiter, who nodded. Though Pete wasn't exactly sure he knew, he nodded anyway, too.

"But I bet you do not know," Felix Serreno continued, "that though the concept was invented by the Greek Hipparus, the design was made perfect by Muslim astronomers and scientists. In particular a woman named Mariam al-Astrulabe."

"As in astrolabe?" Bob asked.

"Wow!" Pete said. "Who knew?"

Still, all of this information was making Pete's head spin, so he was relieved when Mrs. Serreno asked if the boys would be joining the family for lunch. They all said an enthusiastic yes.

"Good!" Felix Serreno said. "In the meantime, please make yourselves at home. Feel free to explore the house and the grounds. Investigate to your hearts' content. Fortunata rings quite a loud bell at lunchtime; I'm sure you won't miss it."

Pete handed Luciano back to Fortunata, who smiled sweetly and thanked him again, and then the three of them were gone, leaving Pete and the boys alone again on the porch with Phillipa.

"They're great!" Pete said.

Phillipa smiled. "I told you," she said. "Now you guys run off and do whatever you want to do. In about twenty minutes, I'm supposed to talk to a colleague of mine about Alessandro Moretti, and I want to be near my computer when I do it."

"It's too nice to go inside right now," Jupiter said. "I think we'll wander around the grounds." Pete suspected he wanted to find the seven sundials Chauncey had told them about the night before – and he did, too. It was time to get down to business and find the hidden treasure!

"Maybe you'll run into Clemente DeLuca," Phillipa said.

"Who's he?" Bob asked.

"A stonemason the Serrenos have hired to do some work. I met him briefly last night. He's quite a character. See you later." She went into the house, leaving The Three Investigators on the porch.

As soon as they started walking, Pete saw three men in the distance shading their eyes and staring in their direction. As they got closer, Pete could see they had been working in a small garden surrounded by a low stone wall in need of repair. Down the center was a gravel path that led to what looked like a stone circle. Off to the side was a large arrangement of carefully stacked blocks.

All three of the men were streaked with dirt and sweat. Pete could see at a glance who was in charge. He was in his forties, about Pete's height but considerably beefier, with a glistening shaved head. His narrow-set eyes squinted beneath gray-flecked eyebrows. He wore work pants and a sleeveless dirty white t-shirt. His biceps were enormous, the kind you saw on the covers of supermarket weight lifting magazines. They almost didn't look real. Around his neck he wore several gold chains, one of which held a small cross that glinted in the sun.

"Ciao!" the bald man said when the boys were still walking toward him. He smiled hugely and spread his arms. "I am Clemente DeLuca," he said, "and these are my *assistenti*, Umberto Mancini and Lorenzo Costa. Lorenzo doesn't speak much English."

Mancini and Costa were younger than Clemente DeLuca, Pete thought. Mancini was heavy-set and heavy-bearded with a thick mustache and jet-black hair. He looked like a tightly coiled spring. Costa was taller and had a foolish grin on his face, as though he didn't quite understand what was going on but was trying to look agreeable.

"You must be the boys Signore Serreno told me about," DeLuca said. "You find missing things?"

"We're The Three Investigators," Jupiter said. He introduced himself, Bob, and Pete.

"I tre investigatori," DeLuca said.

It turned out that a very rich man who owned a winery up the valley had brought DeLuca and Lorenzo Costa over from Italy to rebuild the stonework on his estate. DeLuca had hired three or four American stone masons to help him with the work. So efficient had these stone masons been that Clemente DeLuca and Lorenzo Costa had finished the job early.

Since he still had months left on his visa, Clemente DeLuca had taken the job at Castello Serreno, and although Umberto Mancini hadn't been one of his original American assistants, he had hired him on for the job at Castello Serreno.

"It is a small business," DeLuca said, "but any day working with stone is a good day. Soon – maybe day after tomorrow – we go with il signore and his wife to Sacramento to find the stone I need to finish. Come. I show you."

DeLuca began walking down the gravel path to a perfect circle of stone blocks that had recently been fitted together. It surrounded a floor of white marble, veined here and there with blue and gray. When Pete looked closely, he could see no space between the stones. These guys were very fine workmen.

"It is an old fountain," DeLuca said. "But very small and very simple. Umberto and Lorenzo will rebuild it next week. I am carving an angel holding grapes to put at the top."

He leaned over, picked up a block of stone, and carried it out of the way. His muscles bulged. Pete could hardly believe his eyes. The stone must have weighed over two hundred pounds and DeLuca had picked it up easily.

When DeLuca saw the expression on Pete's face, he turned to him proudly. "Yes," he said. "I am very strong. But I would not hurt a fly.”

“That's good to hear,” Pete said – though privately, he wondered a little why De-Luca had felt the need to say that.

DeLuca's eyes narrowed. “Il signore said you come to look at his house?”

“And to find the treasure!” Bob said cheerfully.

“The treasure?” DeLuca said. “Yes, I have heard the stories. But I have not seen it.” He laughed heartily. “I heard that the treasure was buried by pirates!”

“Pirates?” Jupiter said. “What were they doing so far inland?”

DeLuca looked at Jupiter playfully. “Maybe I am wrong. Maybe it is Spanish gold, stolen from the Indians in Mexico.”

“Do you know where it is?” Pete asked eagerly.

DeLuca looked at him with a big grin. “If I knew where it was, do you think I would tell you?”

“No,” Pete admitted. “Probably not. But do you have any clues?”

DeLuca looked totally innocent – so innocent that Pete had to believe he knew *some-thing*.

“You seem like a good boy,” DeLuca

said to Pete. "Are you Catholic?"

"My parents are," Pete said. "I'm supposed to be."

"It is interesting," DeLuca said, "to be Italian Catholic stonemasons working for Portuguese Muslim hotel-owners."

Pete didn't know what he meant by that, but it *did* sound interesting, somehow.

"There's no treasure here," said Umberto Mancini in a somewhat disdainful way, as he walked down a side path to pick up some tools that had been left there.

His comment made Pete so curious that he followed him down the path and asked him, "Why are you sure?"

"My parents are from Pisa, and before they came to America, their parish priest told them that all the rumors were total nonsense. About the celestial globe that had been made by a Muslim astronomer almost a thousand years ago, and then taken to America." Mancini picked up a rake. "And as a good Catholic, I believe him."

Since Clemente DeLuca had just been talking about Spanish gold and pirate treasure, there was something about this comment that struck Pete as really odd. But before he had time to question Mancini further, he picked up the other rake and a very long shovel and swung back up to the path. There, Jupiter was saying, to Clemente DeLuca, "We were looking for the garden with the seven sundials. Can you direct us?"

DeLuca pointed. "Over there," he said. "We will be getting to the sundials next."

When they were walking up the gravel path, leaving the masons behind, Bob said, "They're very good at what they do."

Jupiter nodded. "What did Phillipa call him? 'Quite a character'? While I'm glad we met him, it took more time than we were allowing. I think we should put off the sundials and go back to the house itself now, or we're not going to have time to see it before lunch."

They let themselves in through the front door and stood in the foyer, looking around. Pete found that he couldn't stop thinking about Clemente DeLuca and the way he had picked up that block of stone. He had been friendly and open enough, Pete thought. Almost too friendly.

Pete reminded himself that Italians were a famously emotional people, but beneath the friendliness was something else. Pete wouldn't call it menace, exactly, but when DeLuca had said that he wouldn't hurt a fly, Pete had a hunch he wasn't being wholly truthful.

Jupiter led the way up a staircase off the foyer. Pete dawdled just a little so that he could bring up the rear. Now that they were officially on the case, he was going to take his responsibility seriously. He was sure there was a hidden treasure in the house, and he was equally sure that, if he looked hard enough, he'd be able to find it.

Could it be behind the wall paneling on one side of the stairs? As quietly as he could, Pete knocked with his knuckles to see if it was hollow, but the sound let him know it was solid.

As they walked through the house, Pete remained on the lookout for a creaky board, a false wall, a closet less deep than it ought to be. This wasn't going to be easy! he thought.

There were so many rooms and windows and flights of stairs that he was afraid he wouldn't be able to keep track of where they'd even looked. The ceilings were so high and the ornamentation so detailed and each room so interesting that he found himself just *looking*. He noticed that many of the rooms had identical built-in cupboards, in the corner near a window. Their doors were about a foot square. He opened several, and every one was empty.

Pete was unexpectedly tired by the time

they clattered down a flight of stairs to the ground floor. Paying close attention was hard work! He found himself in a hall at the back of the house, standing before a set of tall glass French doors.

Jupiter opened them, walked through, and Pete found himself in a room unlike any he had ever seen before. It had been built off the side of the old Victorian, and stood alone, connected to the house only by the wall with the French doors. The three other walls were made of tall glass windows with elaborate leading. Another set of glass French doors opened onto a stone terrace.

"What is this?" he asked. "It's all window!"

"It's called a conservatory," Bob said. "Mostly for growing plants where there was plenty of light. Lots of Victorian houses have them."

Now that he knew what he was looking at, some of the details became clear. The floor was bare stone, the individual pieces fitted carefully together, and over near the glass walls was an array of highly decorative plant stands, made of curved metal, with lots of curlicues and filigrees. Only a few of them had plants in them.

"Look at that!" Pete said. The vaulted ceiling did not rise to a point, but instead to a square flat section, in the very middle of which was a large round skylight.

"Very impressive," Jupiter said. "A true feat of engineering. If that was all glass, it would get too hot in here, so the architect created a solid roof with just the skylight in the middle."

Pete walked over to stand under it, or as close as he could get. He stopped at a low stone wall that formed a circle under the skylight. The wall had been made of flattish stones, very carefully placed, so that no mortar or cement had been used.

"Clemente DeLuca would approve of this," Pete said. "What's that?"

In the center of the circle made by the stone wall was another, much smaller circle holding an elaborate instrument carved of wood. It looked like some of the decorative touches that Pete had seen throughout the house, but this one was fully three-dimensional.

The wood that formed its base was inscribed with lines and arrows, suns and moons. Its rim had been notched into twenty-four equal sections, each with a Roman numeral carved into it, beginning with I and running sequentially to XII, and then starting at I again.

No matter how you looked at it, the same number was at the exact top and exact bottom of the instrument. Over the base another circle had been placed – this one containing yet a third offset circle whose rim had been carved with all sorts of symbols Pete hadn't seen before. On top of all of this was a pointer, like one you'd find on a compass. It looked like each part had been meticulously carved and then all three put together.

"That's an astrolabe," Jupiter said. "But I've never seen a wooden one before."

"They're usually made of metal," Bob agreed.

So that's what an astrolabe was, Pete thought, remembering what Mr. Serreno had said about Mariam al-Astrulabe. It looked complicated.

"That's odd," Jupiter said, pointing to a number of terra cotta pots that had been set on top of the low stone wall.

"Do you think this whole elaborate design was created to show off some special plant or plants?" Bob asked.

"If so," Jupiter said, "they would be plants that tolerated intense and very hot sunlight." He looked up. "At noon, the sun would be close to directly overhead."

Huh, Pete thought. Not so great for plants.

"It's fascinating," Jupiter said. "Look at the floor. Circles within circles." He pointed out how the architect had carefully placed seven round flagstones, arranged in another perfect circle around the outside of the stone wall, but another five feet out. It seemed like the sort of thing that someone would come up with who had designed the calendar house itself − overly elaborate. If it had a purpose or meaning, it was pretty obscure.

"What do you think it means, Jupe?" Pete asked.

"As of now," Jupiter said, "I have no idea. Nor do I understand the design of that." He pointed up at the skylight overhead. For the first time, Pete studied it. It was really pretty cool, like a window to the sky, made up of twelve oblong panes of glass, though wider at the outer ends and tapering toward where they were clustered around a circular pane at the very center. The window looked to Pete like a gigantic sunflower with twelve glass petals.

He looked at Jupiter, who was pinching his bottom lip.

"What is it, Jupe?" he asked.

"I looked carefully at the leaded glass windows throughout the house," Jupiter said. "There's a lot of leading, keeping all the panes in place."

"Three hundred sixty-five of them," Pete said.

Jupiter smiled. "That remains to be seen," he said. "Or rather counted. But that window up there − its leading looks more decorative, somehow, thicker and fancier."

Just then they heard Mrs. Serreno's bell ring for lunch and Pete was immediately hungry. He started for the French doors. The room, impressive as it was, had disappointed him as a place worthy of further exploration. Not only was it the brightest room in the house but there were no walls behind which something could be hidden. Everything was too transparent, too out in the open. The treasure was somewhere else.

"Are you coming?" he asked Bob and Jupe.

"You bet," Bob said.

Jupiter nodded, but as he was about to leave the conservatory, Pete noticed him looking back, an expression of puzzlement on his face. Pete couldn't imagine what he was puzzled about − though he also had the nagging feeling that he himself was forgetting something he had seen or heard or wondered about. He had meant to mention it to Jupiter, but it had slipped his mind for the moment.

8

Suspicions and Clues

As Bob settled in to eat lunch at a table set for eight – the Serrenos, The Three Investigators, Phillipa Paxton, and the man she had told them was writing a book about calendar houses – he found himself thinking about the evening before and, in particular, about what Brother Anders had said about order and chaos.

To Bob, Brother Anders had seemed an odd sort of man to have ended up as a novice in a monastery in the mountains – a man who had run a hedge fund for maybe six or seven years but then had joined the Franciscan order, even though he hadn't even been raised a Catholic. Bob wished he had thought to look up the hedge fund the night before. Maybe he could do it later today.

For now, however, he needed to pay attention to what was going on around him. Phillipa Paxton had arrived at lunch at the final instant, looking flushed and excited, and when Jupiter had asked her how things had gone in her conversation with her colleague, she had said, "Really well. I'll tell you about it later."

150

Now, she was talking to the other historian staying in the house – a man who had introduced himself as Oliver Price. To Bob, he didn't look at all like a historian – more like an aging linebacker. He had broad shoulders and thinning hair combed over his scalp and an odd habit of not looking you in the eye when he talked to you.

And although at first he seemed enthusiastic about talking with the others about Castello Serreno, when he learned that Phillipa was also a historian and was also writing a book about houses, it seemed to Bob that he suddenly got very nervous and guarded. Maybe it was because he was an amateur and Phillipa was a professional, but to Bob, it seemed that Mr. Price had been much more talkative and open before the conversation about calendar houses started.

He'd explained that he'd originally been an accountant and a bookkeeper and was new to both history and writing. But he'd always had a love of and fascination with both houses and astronomy, he said, and when he'd seen a feature article in a Santa Rosa paper about the house – and that it was for sale – he'd come to look at it, even if he knew he could never afford to buy it.

He'd fallen in love with it, he'd said, and afterwards he'd gone home and done a lot of research about calendar houses and thought maybe he could write a book about them. The Serrenos had been good enough to let him stay before the hotel really opened, and when he'd finished his work, he planned to go to Europe and research some other calendar houses.

However, when Phillipa asked him which houses he planned to visit, he had almost nothing to say. He was remarkably vague about where he was going next – which was odd, Bob thought, because it wasn't as though the world was filled with calendar houses.

When they'd finished lunch and Phillipa was helping Mrs. Serreno wash up, Felix Serreno offered to show The Three Investigators his favorite parts of the house. He pointed out the intricate stonework in the floor of the foyer and the elaborate Italianate tiles around the fireplace in the main drawing room. Finally, he took them to the far back corner of the house, where one of the house's towers, with its sharp conical cap, rose above the roofline.

"The house itself has only two floors," Mr. Serreno explained, "but the towers each have three. One of them has been made into a guest room already, but the others haven't."

He climbed the spiral staircase with Bob and the others close behind, and they emerged into a room Bob thought was amazing. As Mr. Serrano had said, the tower jutted above the rest of the house. The room itself was round, with windows evenly spaced on the curved walls, so Bob could see not only the shingles of the roof to one side but panoramas of fields and vineyards, trees and hedgerows.

"Look," Jupiter said, pointing. "Is that the garden with the seven sundials?"

Mr. Serreno came to see what Jupiter was pointing at and told him yes, that was the sundial garden.

"Are there really seven?" Bob asked. "Why so many?"

"There are indeed seven," Mr. Serreno said, "all part of the architect's design, though I do not know their purpose."

"What a cool room!" Pete said.

It was flooded with light. Light streamed in from all the windows, and no part of the room was dim or in shadow, and as Bob looked out on the grounds, he found himself wishing that Mallory were here to see what he was looking at. She would love this so-called castle and its towers, he was sure – and although he now knew that he and she would

153

never be boyfriend and girlfriend, he still missed her more than he had expected to, on this first case of The Three Investigators' new summer.

Still, even if she *wasn't* here – at least not yet – ever since Bob had almost miraculously managed to guess the secret of the ever-shifting passwords devised by Brother Anders, he had been feeling bucked up about both the unexpected accomplishment and himself. Although he'd known for quite a while now that he was good at research, and organization, and even writing, since Jupiter was good at almost *everything*, it was sometimes hard for Bob to feel that his own accomplishments measured up. This time, he was sure they really had.

Meanwhile, Pete was staring at the door to a cupboard in the wall.

"Mr. Serreno," Pete said. "Do you know anything about these cupboards? There are ones like this in almost every room of the house."

"It's an interesting story," Mr. Serreno said. "Giuseppi Donati, the man who had this house designed, was obsessed with fire. He'd built a great house back in Italy, and it had burned to the ground. It bankrupted him, essentially, which is the reason he came to America. When he had this house constructed, he had special fire escape cupboards built into every exterior room on the second or third floor, with knotted ropes that would allow someone to escape through one of the windows. By the time Fortunata and I bought the house, most of the ropes were missing. The few that remained were in pretty bad shape. They didn't look entirely safe."

"So they're all gone now?" Pete asked.

"More or less," Mr. Serreno said. "There may be a few left somewhere."

"I opened a lot of cupboards earlier," Pete said, "and I didn't find any."

Mr. Serreno nodded. "That's what I thought." He smiled at the boys and glanced at his watch. "It is time for me to go back to work. You must be thirsty. Fortunata will have put out lemonade on the terrace. Perhaps you would like some?"

They walked down the circular stairs and through a maze of halls. Bob was glad they had a guide – the house was quite confusing. They found themselves in the conservatory again, and Felix Serreno motioned them toward the French doors that led to the stone terrace. Through the glass walls, Bob could see Phillipa Paxton seated at a round metal table.

"Why, hello!" she called. "Come join

me. I've been wanting to talk to you since before lunch."

Mrs. Serreno had set out a pitcher of lemonade, a number of glasses, and a plate of cookies on an oblong tray. When they all sat down, Phillipa said, "So what did Felix show you? Anything interesting?"

"You bet!" Pete said. "He took us to one of the tower rooms."

"Ah, yes," Phillipa said. "Many Victorians have a single tower, but I don't know of any that has as many as this house does. I forgot to ask you at lunch – did the three of you run into Clemente DeLuca?"

"We sure did," Bob said. "It would have been impossible to miss him. He looked like he was waiting for us."

"I doubt that's the case," Phillipa said, "but he does keep his eyes open."

"I don't know how Jupe and Bob felt," Pete said, "but I thought he was a little shifty."

Bob hadn't felt that way at all.

"What do you mean, Pete?" he asked.

"He seemed really interested in the treasure," Pete said. "Too interested. We need to keep a close watch on him."

"Mostly, I think, we need to take what he says with a few grains of salt," Jupiter said.

"He seems inclined to make things up."

"Like what?" Pete said.

"Like pirates and Spanish gold," Jupiter said.

"I hope not," Pete said. "That's the part of him I liked the most."

"I don't know about Clemente DeLuca," Bob said. "But I'm not sure I trust Oliver Price."

"I couldn't agree with you more," Phillipa said. "Did you see his reaction when he learned that I'm a historian and also writing a book about houses?"

"I thought maybe it was because he's an amateur and you're a professional," Bob suggested. "He's only recently started working on his book."

"It's more than that," Phillipa said. "I've known lots of amateur historians and the one thing they have in common is that they're absolutely passionate about their area of interest. I mean, they know everything, every little detail, and once you get them started, you can't get them to stop. But Mr. Price had almost nothing to say.

"Anyway, all of that can wait. I've got the kind of news I think the three of you are really going to like. I'm not sure *I* like it, mind you. But I think you will.”

“Well, what is it?” Pete asked – forgetting to ask politely in his excitement. “Something about the buried treasure? Something about Alessandro Moretti?”

“Something about both of them at once,” said Phillipa. “The colleague I spoke to today is writing a paper on Moretti, and he told me he’d found a letter in an archive that suggested that Moretti had been killed by the owner of this house and then buried somewhere in the grounds – along with a bag of Spanish gold! The letter was written by the doctor who treated Donati’s wife when she was dying, and although he couldn’t be certain he understood what she was saying correctly – not least because she was speaking partly in Italian! – he thought she was confessing to a crime.”

“A crime in which buried treasure and buried bodies went together,” said Jupiter. “That’s very interesting, when you remember what Brother Anders said last night.”

Wow! thought Bob. That was totally true. But before Phillipa had time to ask what Jupiter was referring to, her cellphone rang, and when she took it out of her pocket and glanced at the Caller I.D., a smile crossed her face.

"It's Mallory MacLeod!" she said, punching a button. "Hello, Mallory!" she said.

Wow! Bob thought for the second time. He'd just been thinking about her!

Phillipa listened for a minute and then asked Mallory to wait. She told the boys that Mallory's father's cousin had managed to change Mallory's reservation so that she could fly to Sacramento rather than back to southern California.

"When will she get here?" Bob asked.

"Tomorrow," Phillipa said.

"That's terrific!" Pete said.

Phillipa punched a button and laid the phone on the table. "You're on speakerphone," Phillipa told her cheerfully and the boys clustered around. For a second there was silence. Then Mallory said, "Hey guys!" Her voice was tinny and far away, but still clearly hers. "How's everything going?"

"Really well," Bob said. "We just got to the calendar house today. The Serrenos are wonderful."

"I can't wait to get there," Mallory said. "The only thing is, I don't know how I'll get from the airport to Napa. But I'll figure it out."

"Why don't I pick you up?" Phillipa said. "It's not that far."

"Really?" Mallory said. "That would be totally great."

"Just give me your flight number and arrival time," Phillipa said. She rummaged in her bag for a notebook and a pen, then wrote down the information. "O.K.!" she said. "See you tomorrow!"

"One last thing," Bob said, "in case you were wondering. We got the letters Phillipa told us about – the ones from Alessandro Moretti, the architect? – and we decoded them. He was writing to a monk named Brother Benedict, and it seems they were both Freemasons. But the letters told us something else – there's definitely something hidden on the property."

"A treasure!" Pete said.

"Don't find it before I get there!" Mallory said.

"Why don't you call me tonight on my cellphone   and I can fill you in on the rest?" Bob said.

"I'll do that!" said Mallory. "Definitely!"

As she hung up, Mallory could hardly have been more excited. She'd spent much of the morning discovering how hard it was to place a cellphone call from her father's first cousin's house on the ocean, and it had seemed like the latest frustration in a frustrating couple of days. She'd been missing Jupiter, Pete, and Bob and the thrill of unraveling mysteries with them, and when she'd discovered what a big city Vancouver was, she'd even found herself missing Rocky Beach.

Not only that, but as she'd long ago discovered, grownups could be a bit boring. At least her father's cousin was, though he was certainly very pleasant. Hamish MacLeod was in his early 40s, tall, with reddish-brown hair and a closely trimmed beard. She wasn't sure what she'd been hoping for – maybe someone with her father's smile or quirky wit or, better yet, his wisdom.

As it had turned out, though, her father's cousin wasn't at all like her father except in one way – he *smelled* familiar, so hugging him had been nicer than expected.

He and his wife Fiona had certainly tried hard to show her and her mother a good time. They'd taken them on a tour of all of Vancouver's most famous attractions – the seawall in Stanley Park, the Capilano Suspension Bridge, the Museum of Anthropology – which Mallory had loved. Back at the house, he'd tried to entertain her by telling stories about her father before she'd been born.

This morning, he'd also inquired about her plans for the summer, and she'd finally gotten up the courage to tell him about the Salvage Yard and The Three Investigators – and also to ask him whether he'd be willing to change her return ticket so that she could stop in Sacramento instead of flying all the way back to Los Angeles.

To her relief, he'd agreed to do it right away, and now she was calling Phillipa to tell her (and the boys) she was coming. She had thought of simply calling Bob, but since Phillipa had offered to let Mallory share her room at Castello Serreno, she'd thought it would only be polite to call her first.

Now, after shutting down her phone, Mallory hurried downstairs and out through the glass doors to the deck that looked over the water. Her father's cousin stood at the gas grill, getting it ready for later; they were having a seafood cookout for dinner.

"Thanks *so* much for changing my ticket," she said to Hamish. "Everything's set! Dr. Paxton is picking me up in Sacramento."

"That's nice of her," Mallory's mother said.

"I'm glad you can join your friends," said

Hamish. "Are they really detectives?"

"Yes," Mallory said. "They're called The Three Investigators. They're getting to be pretty well known. At least in southern California."

"What are they like?" Hamish asked. "Most boys that age aren't really serious about anything other than sports and girls."

"They're pretty unusual," Mallory said. She thought for a minute about how best to describe them.

"Nice young men," her mother said. "Polite and well-mannered."

Mallory grimaced slightly. Though that was true, it was a pretty feeble way to begin giving someone who didn't know them a sense of who they were.

"They're like interlocking pieces of a puzzle," she explained. "Or meshed gears in a well-oiled engine. They've been best friends for so long, it's hard to tell where one of them ends and the next one begins when they're working together. I like each of them individually, and I also like them as a group."

She paused and took a deep breath. "Let's see," she said. "Jupiter Jones is the leader. He's an orphan, and he lives with his aunt and uncle. He's incredibly smart and analytical, not very emotional. I mean, he feels things, but he finds thinking more important. He's the one who came up with the idea for The Three Investigators."

"He does sound quite unusual," Hamish said, "especially for someone your age."

"Pete Crenshaw plays soccer and baseball; he's tall and good-looking and popular. But he's not a jock at all. He's sweet and vulnerable and he has a huge heart. He loves animals." She smiled thinking about him. "He's got so much enthusiasm and energy.

"Bob Andrews is Records and Research for the firm. He's a whiz at finding things out, on the computer and in the library. He's a bit quieter and more shy than Pete and Jupe. I think he's going to be a writer when he grows up. Right now, he's doing a great job of writing up all The Three Investigators' cases and posting them on their website."

"That's interesting," Hamish said. "I'll take a look at that after you leave."

"I think you'll be impressed," Mallory said. "I was. And I don't impress easily."

Hamish chuckled. "Neither did your father. He could be a hard man to please."

For reasons she didn't completely understand, Mallory found that very comforting.

"What are you four working on now?" Hamish asked.

Mallory summarized the current case, mentioning the calendar house and the rumor about hidden treasure. She ended by telling him about Alessandro Moretti's letters, written in the Freemason's cipher.

"The Freemason's cipher?" Hamish said. "It's been a long time since I thought about that. Did you know I'm a Freemason?"

Mallory almost jumped in her chair when she heard this. "Good grief! You're not really?" she asked, incredulously.

"Yes, really, I am," Hamish said. "I was initiated almost twenty years ago now. I love all the symbology and all the rituals. Ritual is really important to human beings, don't you think?"

Why hadn't they talked about this earlier? Mallory wondered. Suddenly her father's first cousin seemed the opposite of boring.

"Yes," Mallory said. "I agree completely. But tell me about the symbology."

"I can only tell you so much," Hamish said, "because we have our secrets."

"I know," Mallory said. "If you told me, you'd have to kill me."

Hamish laughed. "It's not that intense,

actually. Most of the symbolism involves the tools real stonemasons used. Surely you've seen the square and the compass interlocked? And the all-seeing eye of Providence. Everyone has."

Maybe, Mallory thought, but if so she couldn't call it to mind at the moment. Her face must have mirrored her uncertainty, because Hamish jumped to his feet, went into the house, and quickly returned with a book, which he flipped open.

There were the compass and square – the compass with its apex at the top and its two legs opened, the square pointed upwards, its two sides intersecting with the two legs of the compass. Together they formed a space that was roughly square and contained the capital letter G.

Mallory's heart started beating more quickly as she saw at once that the symbol on the grindstone Uncle Titus had brought back from the calendar house and the photograph she'd seen of the one inscribed above the doorway of the monks' observatory had been copied and adapted from the Freemason's symbol.

Her voice cracked with excitement as she asked Hamish what the G stood for.

"For Geometry," he said. "The compass, which is used to draw circles, stands for the eternal realm of the spirit. The square, used to draw angles and lines, stands for the earthly realm, the material."

He flipped another page and showed Mallory a picture of the all-seeing eye of Providence, a large eye from which rays of light streamed in all directions, almost like a corona.

"There's something like that on the American dollar bill," she said.

"That's right," Hamish said. "It's on the back, on the left, in a triangle formed by the top of a pyramid. Often, in Christian iconography, it stands alone, with a defined triangle around the eye. The triangle stands, I would guess, for the tripartite God – Father, Son, and Holy Ghost – with rays of light streaming out from behind the triangle.

"But in our symbology the eye generally stands alone as a reminder that everything humankind thinks and does is observed by the all-seeing eye of God."

"That's totally brilliant," Mallory said.

"Speaking of brilliant," Hamish said, "in the United States, the Eye of Providence is often associated with the Illuminati. Which makes sense, since the Illuminati was founded by a man who was attracted to Freemasonry."

"The Illuminati?" Mallory asked, surprised. "You mean, like in that movie?"

She must have sounded so amazed that Hamish started laughing. "Exactly," he said.

"Hamish," Fiona said. "I think it's time you stopped flipping pages and started flipping seafood."

"Right away," Hamish said. "I will feed the multitudes." He put the book down on a side table and went back to his grill.

Mallory's mother and Fiona began talking about Scotland – the latter telling Mallory's mother how much she and Hamish hoped to visit again soon – but Mallory wasn't paying particular attention. She had begun thinking furiously.

She tried as best she could to remember the symbol that had been revealed on the grindstone when she and The Three Investigators had done the rubbing. It looked sort of like the compass and square that Hamish had shown her, but it had been simplified. The square had been straightened out until it had become a ruler – and the two legs of the compass had been turned into the top of an equilateral triangle. The sort-of square formed by the Freemason's compass and square had become a triangle.

The Freemason's G might well stand for "geometry," but Mallory would take large bets that on the grindstone and the monk's observatory it stood for something else entirely – Galilei Galileo.

It was as if whoever had designed the new symbol – Alessandro Moretti? – had wanted to make a totally new statement and yet, at the same time, to allude to the Freemason's symbol, to remind anyone who saw it what he'd been inspired by.

Why this was so Mallory didn't know yet and wouldn't, she was sure, until she had joined the boys in the Napa Valley. She had a hunch that at the center of this mystery stood not the all-seeing eye of God but the figure of an Italian polymath, inventor, and visionary from the 17th century.

She thought back to the symbols on the grindstone. The triangle with the "G" inside it was at the bottom, and at the top was a circle, with rays streaming from it, like the sun. But there was no single eye of Providence inside it. No. Instead it held four smaller circles – what she and the boys had decided must be the largest moons of Jupiter, which Galileo had discovered in 1610.

And since the corona formed by the rays

really and truly *had* looked like a corona, the symbol as a whole was really the four moons, stark and visible against the shadow of a moon in eclipse.

What, exactly, had the symbols' designer believed in? Mallory wondered. If it was Alessandro Moretti, who had used the Freemason's cipher, had his Masonic beliefs been paramount? Where did Galileo fit in? And what did the monk to whom Moretti had written believe in? Surely his paramount belief had been in God. But maybe not, Mallory thought.

This evening would be torture. Hamish and Fiona had kindly suggested they take a tourist boat out on the ocean, as a treat for their last day. But Mallory knew that she'd be able to think about nothing but the case that was unfolding before her, and how Jupiter, Pete, and Bob were doing. Talk about triangles! Boy, did she wish she was already with them.

Right after dinner, she thought, she'd excuse herself and go to her room and, after she called Bob — and maybe Mrs. Serreno, just to make sure it was really all right with her if she stayed at the castle — she'd get onto her laptop. There was lots of research to do.

Among other things, she wanted to find

out all that she could about the Illuminati. From what she remembered they were a secret society – one so shrouded in mystery that for many years they were only a rumor. Did *they* have something to do with the case?

9

A Mysterious Sundial

It was seven-thirty the next morning when Jupiter, together with Bob and Pete, sat down for breakfast in the monastery's refectory. All three of them were uncharacteristically quiet. There was hardly anyone else in the refectory this morning, but a solemn monk put down a loaf of fresh bread, pots of butter and jam, a pitcher of cream, and bowls of hot porridge with honey.

"They have their own bees, remember," Bob whispered as Pete stirred the honey into his cereal.

"Do they have their own cows, too?" Pete asked.

Jupiter had managed to sleep until almost seven, when the monastery's rooster crowed, but he knew the monks had been up for hours. They had gathered in utter darkness at 4:30 for Vigils, during which they chanted the Psalms. They gathered again for Lauds, at 6:00, to greet the rising sun, and after that they spent time in silent prayer and contemplation.

With only four or five brothers eating

breakfast at the same time they were, the refectory was almost silent, unlike the companionable bustle of dinner the night before. That was fine with Jupiter; in his mind he went over what he hoped to accomplish during the day. Mallory should be arriving around noon or so, but before that they had a lot to get done. The sundial garden was at the top of Jupiter's list — followed by a careful counting of Castello Serreno's rooms and the panes of glass in its windows.

He was now convinced that something connected to Freemasonry was hidden in a secret room in the house, in a secret cupboard, behind a false wall or a sliding panel — perhaps somewhere he hadn't considered.

If there was a basement — even a partial one as he knew had been typical of houses built in California in an earlier era — he wanted to explore it. Or maybe whatever it was had been buried on the grounds, perhaps in one of the gardens. Although he was interested in the story Phillipa Paxton had told them about Mrs. Donati's deathbed confession about the murder of Alessandro Moretti, it was a lot less solid a lead than the two letters Moretti had actually written to Brother Benedict.

Of course, Phillipa's story *had* made Jupiter remember the way that Brother Anders had described San Francisco as having buried bodies and buried treasure side by side. That had seemed like quite a coincidence to Jupiter when he'd first heard Phillipa's story – but after all, those sorts of coincidences were actually very common, and he didn't want to start getting suspicious about things that were actually quite ordinary. It was enough that both Bob and Phillipa were suspicious of Mr. Price, and that both Pete and Phillipa were suspicious of Clemente DeLuca, Jupiter thought with amusement.

At that moment, a familiar voice penetrated his thoughts. When he turned his head to the right, he saw that Brother Anders had come into the refectory and was now standing talking to another monk Jupiter hadn't met. Brother Anders was agreeing that the death of someone named Brother Ambrister – five or six months earlier – had been a sad loss indeed. It seemed that Brother Ambrister had died of complications of the seasonal flu.

"I never met the poor man," Brother Anders said, "but I have heard many tales of his humility and forbearance."

"Many of us were sick," the other monk said, "but thanks be to God we recovered."

"I'm amazed at how vicious and deadly the flu can be," Brother Anders said. "I was reading recently about the epidemic of Russian flu in 1889 and 1890. A million people died. A million! The king of Belgium got it. It was spread by people traveling on trains, which were still fairly new then."

Jupiter looked at Bob and Pete to see if they had also heard this comment, but they were lost in their own thoughts. He himself was struck quite hard by what Anders Bergmann had just said. Those were the exact details Bob had read from the Internet article he'd discovered. What were the odds that Brother Anders's knowledge would match theirs?

Jupiter pinched his bottom lip and stared at the man. Could the record of Bob's Internet searches at the monastery have come to the man's attention? But no, Jupiter thought. That seemed impossible − or at the very least highly unlikely − and furthermore, if the fact that they'd cracked the monastery's password system had been discovered, wouldn't one of the monks have questioned them?

So why had Brother Anders been reading about the Russian flu? One possible explanation could be that Anders had come across the very same letters Alessandro Moretti had written to Brother Benedict and had decoded them himself. After all, the Russian flu was not much in the public consciousness these days. Perhaps the historian who had sent Bob the letters had first found them in the monastery archives, and Brother Anders had also seen them there.

Where *were* those archives, anyway? Jupiter wondered. And what was Anders Bergmann's interest in those letters – if he had one? He'd need to think hard about that; it was a peculiar coincidence – especially taken in conjunction with the other coincidence, the one about the buried treasure and the buried bodies.

Pete scraped the bottom of his bowl and sat back in his chair. "We should get going," he said. "We've got a lot to do today."

Soon, they were packed for the trip into the valley, and as they pulled their bikes from the rack and buckled their helmets, they were surprised to see Chauncey Kit, standing on his pedals, pumping hard up the last bit of road to the monastery.

"Hi!" Chauncey said. "Woo!" He was out of breath.

"I know!" Pete said. "That last stretch is a killer."

"I'm glad I ran into you," Chauncey said. "I was just thinking about you guys. Where did you say you were from?"

"Rocky Beach," Bob said. "Why?"

"What are the odds?" Chauncey said. "I was talking to my mom and dad, and they told me two guys in a red camper van arrived yesterday afternoon from Rocky Beach. Maybe you know them."

Another coincidence, Jupiter thought. Or maybe not.

"Uh oh," Pete said. From the expression on Pete's face, Jupiter knew what he was thinking.

"Did you get a look at them?" he asked.

"Just a quick look this morning," Chauncey said. "One of them is sort of short and chubby and blond?"

"Doesn't ring a bell," Bob said.

"And the other one was pretty tall and gawky, with a bristly crew cut and a really big Adam's apple. He said he was here to explore the calendar house."

Pete slammed a fist into the palm of his left hand. "I knew it!" he said. "Skinny Norris!"

Bob groaned. Jupiter wasn't happy about it either, but what could they do? It was a free country.

"So you *do* know him," Chauncey said. "But I guess you're not looking forward to seeing him."

"He's a pest!" Pete said. "Pretty harmless, but really, really irritating." He turned to Bob and Jupiter. "Gee, guys, I'm sorry. When am I going to learn to keep my big mouth shut?"

"I wouldn't worry about it," Jupiter said. "I don't think he'll get in our way."

"He'd better not," Pete said.

"If we run into him, make sure you act like you're not surprised to see him," Jupiter counseled. "That'll get him. The more we act like he doesn't bother us, the more it will bother *him.*"

They said goodbye to Chauncey and started the long glide down into the valley. On the way, Jupiter kept thinking about Brother Anders. The night before, when they'd gotten back to the monastery and after they'd eaten dinner, they'd only gotten online for half an hour or so and Bob hadn't done any further research about the case – although he'd spent some time talking to Mallory about it.

Still, when Bob was done with his phone call, he and Pete and Jupiter had walked up to the observatory again. There, they'd gotten talking about some things that Jupiter had learned in the year or so since he'd discovered that his father and mother had both been astronomers.

For example, although almost everyone in the world these days believed that Galileo – with help from his friend Copernicus – was the father of the scientific method, in actual fact, Ibn al-Haytham – one of the most famous mathematicians and astronomers of the Islamic empire – was actually the one who first thought of it and promoted it.

Most Westerners had never heard of him, Jupiter had told Pete and Bob, but he had taught that every thinker must be an adversary of received wisdom if he is to find the truth. That you had to be skeptical and ask questions and never believe anything without investigation.

"But that's what you say all the time!" Pete had exclaimed.

After that, they'd spent the evening looking through the telescope and marveling at the stars – and now Jupiter found himself regretting this. He wished they had done some more research about the case. Still, they hadn't, and there was nothing they could do about it now.

It was a pleasant morning, and not too

hot, at least, and the three of them were just about to get to the gravel driveway leading to Castello Serreno when a red camper van pulled out of it, with Skinny Norris in the passenger seat. He was smirking, and clearly looking forward to seeing the boys' surprise and anger as he waved at them in a kind of taunt.

Jupiter hoped that Bob and Pete would remember what he had said and he was happy to see they did. They both called "Hi, Skinny," and waved gaily, as if seeing him had made their day. Skinny thrived on discord, and the look of disbelief, incomprehension, and disappointment on his face as he and his companion sped away was priceless. It was so easy to get the better of Skinny Norris.

No one was on the front porch when they pulled up, and after a brief consultation – sundials or counting? – they decided to visit the garden before the day got too hot. Jupiter knew exactly where the sundial garden was after seeing it from the tower room the day before, and he took off toward it, followed by Pete and Bob. They hadn't gotten too far before they ran into Clemente DeLuca and his two assistants – all of whom seemed happy to see them.

"Buongiorno!" Clemente DeLuca said. "How are you this fine morning?"

"Very well, thank you," Jupiter said.

"We have just met your two friends from – what was it? – Rocky Beach," DeLuca said.

"Yes," Jupiter said. "They're not exactly friends."

"That is not what the tall one said," De-Luca responded. "In fact, I think you might be related. He said he and his friend were the Two Investigators. Like you – but older and more experienced and famous."

Pete moaned and Bob started laughing. Jupiter kept a straight face. "Did he tell you what he was doing here?"

"Same as you!" DeLuca said. "He asked me very many questions about the pirate gold. So I told him. If I were a pirate, I would have buried the treasure among the sundials."

"So he thinks that's where the treasure is?" Jupiter asked. "Do you?"

DeLuca looked playful again. "I am just a poor workman," he said. "What do I know? But I have a feeling. How you say in English – la intuizione."

"Intuition?" Bob asked. "Jupiter calls it reason speeded up."

"Sì!" DeLuca said. "Intuition. I saw an opera once about a treasure buried under a sundial. A poor girl and her father found it and lived happily ever after!"

"Really?" Pete said.

DeLuca nodded solemnly. "In Italy, sundials are everywhere. Very important to my
culture. You cannot walk in any direction without tripping over one. In Firenze, there is magnificent cathedral, La Cattedrale di Santa
Maria del Fiore. Molto bello. Only two
churches in the world are bigger. They say that
is where the Rinascimento – how you say in
English?"

"Renaissance?" Bob suggested.

"Yes!" DeLuca said. "Bravo! That is
where the Renaissance started. At the top of
the dome is an eight-sided window, and on
June 21 – "

"The summer solstice," Jupiter said.

DeLuca nodded vigorously. "On that
day, the sun streams through that window and
falls on a bronze plate that casts a shadow."

"The gnomon," Jupiter said.

DeLuca looked at him curiously. "I do
not know what that means, but never mind.
There is also a famous sundial in the Duomo di
Milano, the dome of the cathedral in Milan.
The beam of light moves over a fancy strip of
metal on the cathedral floor. I have heard it
works perfectly."

Jupiter found all of this very interesting. But DeLuca was just warming to his subject. He went on to talk about the Obelisco di Montecitorio in Rome, a red granite obelisk made in Egypt five hundred years before the birth of Jesus Christ. It had first been in the city of Heliopolis –

"City of the sun," Jupiter said.

According to DeLuca, the obelisk had been brought to Rome by the first Roman Emperor Augustus, who had used it as the gnomon of the Solarium Augusti, the largest sundial of the ancient world, in the Campus Martius.

"Augustus?" Pete asked. "Why is that name so familiar?"

"Because of August August and the plaster bust of Octavian, remember?" Bob said. "Octavian and Augustus were the same person."

"The Fiery Eye!" Pete said. "Of course! I was thinking about Dial Canyon!"

Jupiter nodded. "There seems to be some odd connection between sundials and jewels."

"Now you're talking!" Pete said. "Doesn't Octavian have something to do with 'eight'?"

"Indeed," Jupiter said. "Which is why August is the eighth month."

"There sure are a lot of numbers flying around in this case," Pete said. He sounded aggrieved. "Three hundred sixty-five, fifty-two, twelve – "

That was true, Jupiter thought. And seven. Seven days of the week, seven sundials, seven round flagstones in the conservatory. Which, Jupiter thought, also had a skylight set at the top of the vaulted ceiling. Different from the ones in the cathedrals that DeLuca had told them about. But still –

"Thank you very much, Mr. DeLuca," Jupiter said. "It's been a pleasure talking with you, and you've been very helpful."

"Grazie!" DeLuca said. "Buongiorno."

The sundial garden was some distance from the main house and was clearly a part of the grounds which had not yet been attended to by the Serrenos. He and his friends entered through a lavish arbor twined with flowering vines and saw four ragged and weedy perennial borders forming its perimeter – two of them filled with roses in full bloom – and a central field of meadow grass in which the sundials must be hidden.

Coming closer, Jupiter could see that the

seven sundials were arranged not in a straight line of ascending size, or randomly placed, but in a circle in the center of the garden. The smallest sundial was very small indeed, about the size of a large teacup's saucer, and the gnomon rose only an inch or two above the horizontal plate. The next biggest one was perhaps the size of a dinner plate, with a correspondingly higher blade.

The circle in which the sundials were arranged looked asymmetrical due to their increasing size, but though Jupiter couldn't be sure, it seemed to him that if you drew a line on the ground that went through the center point of each of the brass plates you'd wind up with something approximating a perfect circle.

At the moment, some of the smaller sundials were choked with grass, and the largest one was covered with a weedy sort of vine, but Jupiter could imagine that when they were cleared off, they would make a very restful impression on the mind.

"Boy," Bob said. "This is really something! Do you think Alessandro Moretti designed this garden?"

"I don't know," Jupiter said. "But there's every reason for us to believe he designed the sundials." He bent over and cleared away a surface. "Look at this one – it's an exact replica of the sundial in the monastery garden, and we know from the letter he wrote to Brother Benedict that he designed that one."

He walked over to one of the larger sundials and peered down at its brass plate. "And there's an astrolabe engraved on the bottom of this one – just like one of the carved astrolabes we saw in the house yesterday."

The boys fanned out and started examining the sundials' central plates. The largest sundial had a face that was so overgrown with a creeping vine that they would have had to actually tear it out of the ground to see what lay beneath it, but with just a little light clearing, the other sundials could be seen. All of them were engraved with astronomical symbols. One had a crescent moon. Another had an engraving of what looked like a comet streaming across the sky, with its tail of fire. But why seven sundials, when one would do? Jupiter wondered.

He wished he could see the surface of the largest sundial. It was very big indeed – so large that its base had been constructed not of one but of several marble blocks. The central plate was almost six feet in diameter.

Jupiter was sure he could have lain

across it with room to spare on either end of him, if it hadn't been for the gnomon which was positioned on the radius made by the 12 o'clock line, with its angled point at the center. The gnomon was an ornate and curlicued metal triangle that rose so high above the plate, it had to be two and a half feet tall.

The bottom half of the sundial's plate was the only part other than the gnomon that wasn't concealed by the vine, and on *that* there was a symbol for earth – a circle with a cross at its top – and what Jupiter thought must be symbols for the other planets as well. Marking the center and cut in half by the gnomon's length was a beautifully rendered sun, a foot in diameter, surrounded by a flaming corona.

The rest of the face of the sundial was obscured, but Jupiter could see that the rays of the sun's corona were wider at one end than at the other – the oblong ends set around the sun while their tapered ends pointed toward the Roman numbers that marked the hours spaced around the circle's circumference. Because of the latitude of the Napa Valley, the hours close to noon bunched together while the hours toward dusk and dawn were set more widely apart.

Jupiter called Pete and Bob over.

"Look at that!" Pete exclaimed. He checked his watch and then looked at the shadow cast by the monumental gnomon. "It's pretty close."

Jupiter looked at his watch and then at the shadow. Pete was right. Jupiter's watch read eleven-thirty-two and the shadow was moving toward noon. But he saw clearly that as the sun passed its zenith and the morning became afternoon, the time would be off by greater and greater amounts.

This sundial had not been constructed in order to tell time. In fact, it made no pretense of doing that. It was purely decorative. Its size should have enabled Moretti to make it more accurate, but instead he'd designed it to be less accurate, in terms of telling time, than the smaller sundials in the circle.

The other sundials spaced the hours from six a.m. to six p.m. in a semicircle, with 12 noon at the apex. But this one had the face of a clock. It had been a lot of work for something that had no function at all. It was a mystery to him.

"Boy!" Pete said. "I hope they didn't bury the treasure under this sundial. Or the body. Do you think Alessandro Morreti could be buried under this stone, Jupe? I don't think even Clemente DeLuca could lift it without help. It'd take a piece of heavy machinery to move that thing!"

"It would indeed," said Jupiter.

"I don't think Mr. and Mrs. Serreno would be too happy about that," Bob said. "Particularly since we have no idea what we'd find."

"I doubt it would be a body," said Jupiter. "The apparently guilty ramblings of a sick and dying woman, reported by her doctor, are not what I would call evidence of a crime. We have to guard against the temptation to believe everything we hear. Alessandro Moretti's letters to Brother Benedict are real evidence – evidence that the architect of this house had designed – or was designing – something somewhere which contained items both he and Brother Benedict had an ardent interest in.

"Those items, he said, would soon have a 'hidden home' in a public house he was designing," Jupiter continued. "While we can't know for certain that the house was Castello Serreno, since he only designed three other houses – all of them in San Francisco – the odds are good that the 'hidden home' was in the house behind us. As for Alessandro Moretti's disappearance, for all we know, he died of the Russian flu later the same year he wrote the letters. Whatever this sundial is for, I truly doubt that it's a gravestone."

At these words, Pete looked disappointed, but in very short order he brightened. "Then let's get counting," he said. "The windows *and* the rooms!"

"I also want to ask the Serrenos if they have any plans to clear off these sundials, or if DeLuca and his assistants are supposed to check and repair them," Jupiter said. "I'd like to get permission to come back and clear the vine off the biggest sundial, just so that we have the total picture."

They started walking back toward where DeLuca was working. The sun was climbing, and in Italy, Jupiter thought, if DeLuca was right, a shaft of sun would soon be streaming in through the octagonal window in Florence's cathedral.

DeLuca was an interesting character, Jupiter thought – indeed, that was the word Phillipa Paxton had used to describe him. Jupiter didn't think of him as a liar, but more of a fabulist, a teller of tales. Why would a simple stonemason from northern Italy know anything about Italian opera? Perhaps even more to the point, why would he know the details about a window in a Florence cathedral, thought to be the birthplace of the Renaissance?

But then, Jupiter thought, a cathedral might be of intense interest to a master stonemason.

Still, all four of DeLuca's references – to the opera, the two cathedrals, and the obelisk in Rome that had originally been the gnomon for a sundial – seemed remarkably sophisticated.

Had Pete been right to be suspicious of DeLuca the first time they had met him? Was there, perhaps, more to DeLuca than there had first seemed? The longer he and the others were on the grounds of Castello Serreno, the more Jupiter felt that there were villains about somewhere. It was strange not to know who they were, or what they might be up to.

10

A Meditation Upon A Missing Room

By the time they'd gotten back to the house, Pete's disappointment at Jupiter's speech about the unlikeliness of the sundial garden as a possible hiding place for either a treasure or a body had started to wane. For a moment, he'd been excited at the idea, but Jupe was right that the letters from Alessandro Moretti had been pretty clear that the "items" – whatever they were – were to be hidden in a house.

And after all, even though there was also a lot of talk in the letters about light illuminating darkness, and folding back the cloak of night, if *he* had to hide something precious, Pete thought, he'd want to hide it in the light and air, not under the ground, which was cold, and wet, and where things could happen you couldn't see.

Of course, if it was hidden, you couldn't see what was happening to it anyway, no matter where it was. Still, inside the house was a better bet than in the sundial garden. Pete was leading the way up the porch steps when the front door of Castello Serreno opened and

Mrs. Serreno and Luciano came through it. Luciano was wearing short pants and a bright orange shirt, and Mrs. Serreno had on a wide-brimmed straw sun hat.

"Hello," she said. "So nice to see you all again!"

Luciano gave a cry of pleasure as he saw Pete. He toddled over as Pete hunkered down to be on the boy's level. Luciano's cheeks were bright red, flushed from exercise or emotion, and he stuck out a finger and pointed right at Pete's nose.

"Pit," he said.

Pete laughed. "That's right! Peeete."

"Pit," Luciano said.

Pete grabbed the boy under the arms and hoisted him up, then tossed him into the air. Luciano screamed with delight. "More!" he said. "More!" Pete tossed him again.

Mrs. Serreno smiled. "May all our guests be so good with children," she said.

Pete had now cradled Luciano against his hip, and the boy was busy playing with Pete's hair. It made him feel good that the boy had taken to him, and that Mrs. Serreno had noticed. He'd had lots of practice with his cousins, but he had to admit he really did like children and was surprised that not everyone shared his enthusiasm.

"How is everything going with your search for the treasure?" Mrs. Serreno asked.

Something about her voice made Pete look at her closely, and he guessed, from the expression on her face, that Phillipa Paxton had told her about the letter from Mrs. Donati's doctor – the one which suggested that Alessandro Morreti had been murdered.

Jupiter clearly guessed this, also. "I gather that Dr. Paxton has told you about her conversation with her colleague?" he asked.

"Yes," said Mrs. Serreno. "And although I don't want to believe it, it is hard to put out of my mind."

In response, Jupiter basically repeated what he had said in the sundial garden – that he didn't consider the ramblings of an ill or dying woman evidence of any crime.

He also told Mrs. Serreno about the letters Alessandro Morreti had written to Brother Benedict at the Mountain Monastery. Pete was puzzled by this at first, because, in general, when they were actively pursuing a lead, Jupiter liked to play things close to the chest.

But since the Serrenos would be the owners of any treasure they *did* find in the walls or the floors of the house, Pete saw why Jupiter was breaking his general rule. Mrs. Serreno looked both relieved and highly intrigued at the news.

"Well!" she said. "Those letters are the first solid evidence I've heard in support of the rumors. And it's interesting that Brother Benedict was a Freemason – and apparently a free thinker. Some brothers who keep the monastery garden come down on a regular basis to sell us fruits and vegetables, and although I don't know much about Catholic monks, they seem to be quite traditionally religious. Or at least two of them do. The third is a little different. He seems to be interested in architecture."

Since Pete had gotten the impression that only Brother Benedict and Brother Gerald were involved in the market garden aspect of the monastery, he was surprised to hear about a third monk.

"There are three that come here?" he said, shifting Luciano across his chest.

"Not all at the same time," said Mrs. Serreno. "Just two at a time, but last week the third one was here. He looked so much like one of the other two – I am embarrassed to say I do not know their names – that at first I thought he was the one who had been here before. But then he asked if he could look around the kitchens, and the pantries, and when I heard his voice, I saw at once that he was a different man."

"Brother Anders," said Jupiter thoughtfully. "We've met him. In fact, we've met all three of them, I think. Brother Anselm, Brother Gerald, and Brother Anders. Brother Anders has just recently converted to Catholicism and used to be a hedge fund manager," he explained.

"A hedge fund manager?" exclaimed Mrs. Serreno in amazement. "He gave no hint of that! If I had to guess, I would have thought he was an architect – or perhaps another architectural historian – before he became a monk."

"That's very interesting," Jupiter said. "Did he ask you anything in particular about the house?"

"He asked me about the basement," Mrs. Serreno said. "He said that the monastery has an orchard, and that in the autumn they will have many apples. He asked if the basement might be cool enough to keep them."

"Does the house *have* a basement?" Jupiter asked. "We're about to take you and your husband up on your offer to let us count all the windows and rooms in the house."

"Yes," Mrs. Serreno said, "but it's only a partial basement and not very interesting compared to the rest of the house. The door to it is in the hall behind the kitchen. I don't think it's worth your time. Better you look at the library, which is a beautiful room. The architect's original blueprints are there, in a leather portfolio. And don't miss the wonderful secret passage between the library and one of the sitting rooms. Be sure to look for it."

A secret passage! Pete thought. "Gee," he said. "Thanks. We will!"

"By the way," said Jupiter, "would it be all right with you if we cleared some of the vines away from the face of the largest sundial in the formal garden? We were wondering whether maybe the Italian stonemasons plan to do some work on it. At the moment, you can't see the middle of the stone at all."

"I'm sure that would be fine," said Mrs. Serreno, smiling. She moved toward Pete and gently took her son.

"Where are you off to?" Bob asked.

"My morning stroll," Mrs. Serreno said, "though I'm getting a late start. I like to make sure Luciano gets plenty of sun every day. And I need to speak to Mr. DeLuca. We're all supposed to go to a quarry tomorrow so we can pick out the stone he needs to finish his work."

She put Luciano down and grabbed his hand. With his free hand, he pointed at Pete again. "Pit!" he screamed.

Everybody laughed.

"I'm glad I ran into you," Mrs. Serreno said. "Since Mrs. Paxton is off picking up your friend in Sacramento, lunch will be a little later today – closer to two. I hope that's all right."

Pete's stomach growled, but he said, "That's fine!"

"Now we must be going," Mrs. Serreno said, "or lunch will turn into dinner! I'll look forward to seeing you all in an hour or two."

"Great!" Pete said. He watched as Mrs. Serreno walked down the steps, helping Luciano, and took off in the direction of the sundial garden. Then they entered the house.

"Let's try the basement first," Jupiter said. "Mrs. Serreno may be right that it's not worth our time. But she may be wrong."

Pete agreed with Jupiter. He had high hopes for the basement.

As it turned out, it was dark down there, but dry. A lone light bulb illuminated the space, which was indeed a partial basement stretching under the kitchen and dining room. It held the house's furnace and mechanicals, without much room left over for anything else. Around its perimeter was a solid stone wall. There were no hiding places, either obvious or not. Pete was disappointed. The basement was a bust. No windows. Could this even be called a room?

He asked Jupiter.

"That's a good question," Jupiter said. "We don't know Alessandro Moretti's or Giuseppi Donati's definition of a room. But I think we ought to write the basement down for the time being. Bob?"

Bob had a notebook and a pencil and was ready to inventory every room and the number of panes of glass in its windows. "Got it, Jupe," he said.

They went back upstairs and into the kitchen. Pete was pleased to note that something was cooking in the oven, and it smelled great!

"In here," Bob said. He'd discovered an elaborate butler's pantry with four wide cupboards – each one with shelves laden with staples like flour and sugar and bottled and canned goods. Each also had a multi-paneled door, a square wrought-iron knob, and a window at the top.

"They're just like little rooms!" Pete said, peering into one of them.

"Indeed they are," Jupiter said. "I think they qualify. Bob, what do you think?"

"We could make a rule," Bob said, "that if it has a window it's a room, and if it doesn't, it isn't.'"

"So the rope cupboards don't count," Pete said.

"No," said Jupiter. "So inventory all these 'rooms', and remember to cross off the basement. I think you have to call the space that contains all these little rooms a room as well."

Bob counted the cabinets – four – and the pantry itself – five.

From the kitchen, they headed to the library. Pete looked around at the interior. It had to be thirty feet long and twenty feet wide, with large beautifully tiled fireplaces at each end. The exterior wall held ten very tall windows with decorative leading that looked out on expanses of lawn. The ceiling was nine or ten feet high and its borders were festooned with garlands of plaster flowers.

This was more like it, Pete thought. Who knew what could be hiding behind all those shelves of books?

Two dark tables were set next to each other in the room's center, each one surrounded by comfortable-looking leather-bound club chairs. Pete imagined fires burning merrily in the grates on a wintry day. He glanced at the books and saw that a lot of them were heavy and ornate, with gold leaf on the covers, highlighting words like "Treatise" and "A Meditation Upon" and "Discourse Concerning." Their tops were very dusty.

"The Serrenos sure have a lot of books!" he said to Bob and Jupiter. "There must be thousands and thousands."

"The books came with the house," Bob told him. "Many of them date back to when the house was built."

So that's why there were those fancy old-fashioned words, Pete thought. As he stood looking around him, Jupiter went to a glass-topped display case, opened the lid, and withdrew a leather-bound portfolio. He took it to one of the tables and opened it. Since Bob was now busily counting windows, Pete was alone when he joined him.

Looking over Jupiter's shoulder, Pete saw that the plans for the house had been drawn on large sheets of paper, two feet by three feet, and carefully folded. They were real blueprints – the paper was a deep textured blue crossed by spidery white lines – and there were many of them.

"Look at these elevations," Jupiter said. "They're amazing."

Pete found himself staring at drawings of the house from the front, the back, and each of the two sides.

"Wow!" he said, noting all the decorative flourishes that had been reproduced on the house itself. There were floor plans of each of the building's two floors as well as enlarged plans of many of the rooms.

"Alessandro Moretti sure was a good draftsman," he said.

Jupiter found the plan for the library itself, and Pete noted how carefully Moretti had drawn elevations of the room's four walls, with particular attention to the fireplaces and the exterior wall with the leaded glass windows. Jupiter was continuing to study the blueprint of the library when he made an exclamation of surprise.

"What is it, Jupe?" Pete asked him. "Did you find it!" His voice rose in excitement.

"If you mean the secret passage, yes, indeed," Jupiter said. "I'm surprised Moretti included it on the blueprint. That doesn't make it so secret."

He pointed with his finger at the right

hand side of the eastern fireplace, where the drawing showed a section of wall that seemed to swivel.

"Come on," Jupiter said. "Moretti even drew in the release mechanism. It's a metal lever." He went to the wall with the fireplace, reached up, and fumbled around behind some books that shielded it from view.

Noiselessly, the section of shelves swung back, revealing a dark hallway, not very long, windowless, and about five feet wide.

"Too cool!" Pete said, staring in. "This is so slick!"

"I don't think this had any real purpose," Jupiter said, "other than as a shortcut to get out of the library and into another room. It seems to me a great deal like the sundial gar-den – built merely to amuse the architect and Mr. Donati."

"I like it," Pete said. What better place to hide treasure than a secret passage? he thought.

"Me too," Bob said. "I'm done with counting the windows. Let's go through. Did anyone bring a flashlight?"

"It's very short," Jupiter said. "I don't think we'll need one."

The passageway was narrow and dusty,

and though Pete could walk in without having to bend, his head came close to the ceiling. He followed Jupiter. In no time, Jupe had reached the opposite wall. He felt around with his fingers until he found a lever like the one in the library and switched it.

This time a door slid sideways into the wall. Pete was surprised to see that the passage was still blocked. "What's going on?" he asked.

"It's a tapestry," Jupiter said, "hanging on the wall to cover the entrance." He pushed the fabric out gently and then sidestepped. Pete followed him, doing exactly what he had done.

He found himself in a brightly lit room he'd been in before. It was the main drawing room, where Mr. Serreno had pointed out the ornate tile work around the fireplace. Pete could see it had been positioned on the other side of the wall from one of the library's fireplaces and shared the same chimney. Several tall narrow windows, like the ones in the library, looked out over the same lawn, and a number of elegant chairs and sofas, upholstered in bright sleek colors, stood ready to receive guests. Bob started counting panes of glass again and, this time, so did Pete.

"Do we count that secret passage as a room?" Pete asked.

"I don't think so," Bob said, "if we stick to our rules. No windows, therefore no room. I wish that Mallory were with us already. She'd be a big help with these decisions. What time is it, anyway? When I talked to her last night, she said she thought that she and Phillipa would be able to get here by 1:00 if they were lucky.

"She also said that Mrs. Serrreno was going to give her her own room – that when she heard that Dr. Paxton had offered to share hers, she wouldn't hear of it. Mrs. Serreno said that since the hotel wasn't even really open yet, there was no reason she shouldn't stay in the tower room that's been turned into a bedroom."

"It's only 12:30," said Pete. "And I'm hungry already."

"We'd better get cracking, then," said Bob. "Let's save the conservatory for last and do the second floor next."

There, they worked swiftly from one end of the house to the other. It all went quite smoothly except when they entered one of the larger but still unfinished bedrooms and were surprised to find the amateur historian, Mr. Price, on his hands and knees with a large measuring tape.

"Why, hello!" Mr. Price said. "I was just

wishing I had some help. Would one of you give me a hand?"

Both Jupiter and Bob looked reluctant, but Pete said, "Sure. What do you need?"

"I'm just trying to get the measurements right," Mr. Price said, "and this room is so much bigger than most. Maybe you could hold the tape against the far wall?"

Pete took the metal-tipped end that Mr. Price handed him and walked to the other side of the room, pulling the tape behind him as he went.

"Just hold it steady on the floor, if you would," Mr. Price said. "O.K., I got it," he added. He was kneeling exactly opposite Pete, holding the tape measure against the wall. "Thanks!"

"Why are you taking these measurements?" Pete asked. He suspected that the man was looking for numbers that didn't add up, that would indicate a false wall or concealed compartment, some secret hiding place.

To Pete's surprise, that was exactly what Mr. Price said.

"Well," he said, "I'm a bit ashamed to admit it, but I'm not really a historian in the sense that Phillipa Paxton is. And the book I'm planning to write won't be about a lot of different calendar houses, just this one. I'm aiming for a market of readers who like stories about hidden treasures. And wouldn't it be great for the Serrenos if I actually found one? Better me than Clemente DeLuca. I saw him earlier and he had all sorts of theories about where the treasure might be hidden. But he made me very suspicious."

"What did he say?" Pete asked, gratified to find that his feelings about the stonemason were shared by someone else.

"He said he thought the treasure was buried in the sundial garden," Mr. Price responded, "but, of course, if he was looking for it too, that would just be a bit of classic misdirection."

"Hah!" said Pete. " I knew it! He told us the same thing!"

Bob was done with counting the windows, so the three of them nodded to Mr. Price and left. They checked out the rest of the rooms on the second floor and then descended to the first floor and finished all of the rooms except for the conservatory. Even as Pete hurried, his eyes raked the walls and floors and ceilings, looking for any sign of a secret hiding place, but he saw nothing promising. This treasure hunt was proving unexpectedly difficult.

At last they were finished with everything but the conservatory – which turned out to be a good deal of work. There were a lot of windows! They each counted, quickly, and when they discovered they didn't all agree, they counted again. When they had done their best to get it right, they moved next door, to the drawing room where the tapestry hung. There, Jupiter sat on the edge of a chair and Pete drummed his fingers on a table next to the sofa he was sitting on, while Bob sat next to him and double-checked through his inventory, adding up the number of rooms and windows.

When he was done, he sat back with a puzzled expression on his face.

"Not wholly satisfactory," he said.

"What do you mean?" Pete asked him.

"We only found fifty-one rooms," Bob said. "Not fifty-two."

Jupiter pinched his bottom lip. "Perhaps we were wrong in not counting the rooms with no windows. After all, it was an arbitrary decision."

"So if we include the secret passage, we come to fifty-two?" Pete said.

Jupiter shook his head in exasperation. "I really don't see how you could call that a room," he said.

"We looked everywhere," Bob said, "and pretty carefully. I'm sure I didn't make any mistakes with the inventory. I just don't see how we could possibly have missed a whole room."

"No," Jupiter admitted. "I think you're right. And we certainly saw no indication that there was a hidden room anywhere in the house."

"What about the basement?" Pete asked.

"We could call that a room," Jupiter said, "which would get us to fifty-two. But I just don't feel right about that. When you're counting rooms in a house, you never count the basement."

"Here's the thing," Bob said. "We've got an even bigger problem with the windows. We were expecting to find 365 panes of glass and it's not even close." He looked down again at his notebook to double-check his figures. "We each agreed on the number of panes in each room, and I'm sure I added everything right. I came up with 346. We're missing nineteen panes of glass, which is really a lot."

Now Jupiter looked really aggravated. "I'm sorry to say that throws everything into doubt."

"Maybe not," Pete said. "What if there

really is a hidden room, and it has nineteen panes of glass in it?"

"That would solve our problem," Jupiter said. "On the other hand, if there are only 51 rooms and 346 panes of glass, maybe this isn't a calendar house after all."

"If that's so, then Mallory's going to be very disappointed," Bob said.

"Maybe the number of rooms and panes of glass don't matter," Pete said. "We know for sure that something is hidden inside a cloak of darkness. That's from Alessandro Moretti's letter."

"You're right," Bob said. "And really what we're trying to do is find that treasure, not prove that this is a calendar house."

Jupiter's face lost all trace of irritation. "Both of you are right. And that gives me an idea. Since Brother Colin told me this morning that Father John is supposed to be back at the monastery this evening, maybe tomorrow Mallory can come up to the monastery and we can spend the day searching the archives there. Maybe there are other letters we don't know about."

"Or maybe Brother Benedict kept a journal or a notebook," Bob said.

"Wow! How great would that be!" Pete

said.

Just then, he heard a car on the gravel and looked out the drawing room windows to see that Phillipa Paxton had returned. As the boys started to scramble to their feet, Pete saw Mallory emerging from the passenger seat, her red hair glinting in the sun. She stared up at Castello Serreno in amazement and Pete found himself rushing to a window and throwing it open.

All morning, he'd had the feeling that something was about to happen – though he hadn't been sure what. Now, he wondered if his feeling had just been about his knowledge that Mallory would be arriving soon. Ever since she'd joined The Three Investigators the summer before, he'd been amazed by the way she could see things, and remember things, that other people couldn't.

"Hello!" he called. "We'll be right out! And have we got a mystery for you!"

11

A Midnight Raid

Mallory had known from the pictures of Castello Serreno that it would be a beautiful place, but she hadn't known before she arrived just how pleased she'd be to see Bob and Jupiter and Pete again. As they burst out a door and headed for Phillipa Paxton's car, they looked sunburned and vital and fully alive – and almost as glad to see her as she was to see them. Pete in particular seemed happy to see her – and although she was happy to see them all, she had to admit she was most excited to see Jupiter.

She hoped he'd be impressed with the research she'd done the night before – research about the all-seeing Eye of Providence and the Illuminati. After she'd called Bob and Mrs. Serreno – who'd been really nice in offering to let her stay in her own room – she'd gotten onto the Internet and found out a lot of fascinating stuff about the elusive group.

She'd thought of telling some of it to Dr. Paxton on the drive from Sacramento, but she'd held back so that she could tell The

Three Investigators first. Now, as she saw them, she felt a fresh burst of energy.

"I've got so much to tell you!" she said.

"How was your visit with your father's cousin?" Pete asked. He grabbed the larger of her two bags and hoisted it onto his shoulder.

"Pretty good — particularly at the end when I found out he was a Freemason," Mallory said, grinning broadly. "I think I may have figured out what the symbol on the grindstone and on the keystone of the monastery's observatory means."

Both Pete and Bob's faces lit up, but Jupiter only said, "Indeed? I don't want us to discuss the case in front of the Serrenos or Oliver Price, but we may have time to fill one another in before lunch. Why don't the five of us sit on the porch until Mrs. Serreno rings the bell?"

Mallory grabbed her computer bag and carried it with her to the porch where she put it next to her backpack and sat down between Pete and Bob. Soon the others were sitting staring at her expectantly. Even Jupiter, she was happy to note.

"Well," she said, "I was doing research on the Bavarian Illuminati — "

"The Illuminati!" Phillipa said. "The four of you never cease to amaze me!"

"The Illuminati?" Pete asked. "Like in that movie?"

"Exactly!" Mallory said. "Well, not quite. Although I'd always thought it was basically made up, it turns out the Illuminati was actually real. It was founded in May 1776 – at a time when Bavaria was a whole country of its own – by a man named Adam Weishaupt. Its name means 'the enlightened ones,' and although Weishaupt had originally wanted to be a regular Freemason, eventually he decided to start his own secret society – one whose members believed in rationality and who opposed superstition, and in particular, opposed the influence of religion in government, politics, and public life."

The three boys and Phillipa Paxton were all looking at her attentively. Although she and her mother had gotten up very early to make their flight and it had already been a long day for her, she found their attention both energizing and flattering. It felt good to be back with people she really understood, and she was relieved to have figured out how to join them while the first case of the summer was still in progress.

"They envisioned a state ruled not by the church but by scientists and philosophers who questioned received knowledge and used scientific method," she continued. "I read that several members were fervent disciples of Galileo."

"Yikes!" said Pete.

"Because their beliefs threatened the Catholic Church, the Bavarian Illuminati and other secret societies were outlawed soon after their founding – forcing them underground. The thing is, because Adam Weishaupt had been involved with the Freemasons before he founded the Illuminati, a lot of the Freemason symbols became Illuminati symbols, too. I mean, the guy just borrowed and changed them."

"That makes sense," Phillipa said.

"Then I wondered if maybe there was a connection between the Bavarian Illuminati and Guiseppi Donati or Alessandro Moretti – if either of their families had any German ancestors," Mallory said. "That might explain how some very similar symbols got on the grindstone and the observatory."

She paused to gather her thoughts. "You remember the genealogy website Bob used last summer to research first Isabella Chang's family and then Jupiter's? Well, I re-subscribed to it, then started a new family tree, with Giuseppi Donati and Alessandro Moretti on it, and though it took a little digging, I followed the hints the website gave me and discovered that one of their ancestors had moved to Italy from Bavaria in 1784 – soon after the Illuminati were outlawed by the Duke of Bavaria! Remember that Donati and Moretti were cousins. They had the same ancestor."

"Was the ancestor a member?" Phillipa asked.

"There's no way to know for certain. At least not yet," Mallory said. "But the clues point in that direction. The ancestor's name was Andreas Ritter and he was an engineer. He changed his name to Cavaliere and married an Italian woman and had three children. That's as far as I've gotten in my research."

"Why did he change his name?" Phillipa said.

"He was just translating his name from German to Italian," Mallory said. "Both Ritter and Cavaliere mean 'knight.' I can't prove it beyond a doubt – not yet – but it looks to me like one of the members of the Bavarian Illuminati wanted to be closer to the birthplace of Galileo – one of his heroes. I think the triangle with the "G" in it on the grindstone and the observatory may go all the way back to the Illuminati, and that the 'G' doesn't stand for either 'God' or

'Geometry,' but for 'Galileo,' just as we sort of guessed."

Just then, the bell rang for lunch. "I really did have time you fill you in!" Mallory said. "But you didn't have time to do the same for me. I suppose I can wait until after lunch."

She didn't really want to, though; she wanted to know what Pete had meant when he said, "Have we got a mystery for you!"

Lunch was delicious, and Mallory was delighted to meet Mr. Serreno, a courteous and handsome man with a warm smile, and the Serreno's son Luciano, who clearly had a huge crush on Pete. Mallory was surprised by how beautiful Mrs. Serreno was, and she thanked her again for giving her a room of her own.

After lunch was over, Mallory and the boys went up the staircase toward the bedroom Mrs. Serreno was calling the Tower Bedroom – with Pete still carrying Mallory's larger bag. He was such a *boy*, she thought. A really great boy, and a really thoughtful one. To get to the tower room, they all climbed a short spiral wooden staircase, and when she saw the room, Mallory gasped. It wasn't entirely renovated yet, she noticed – the doorknob seemed loose, and the door hadn't been scraped and repainted yet – but inside there were two extra-long twin beds, some chairs in front of the windows, and a fantastic view of the lawn and gardens.

She felt very lucky. She would have been happy to share with Phillipa, but this was better. As an only child, she'd never truly grown accustomed to sharing a room with someone else, and she always did her best thinking when she was alone. After she had put her bags on the floor next to the bureau, she said, "All right. What, exactly, is the mystery?"

"Why don't we tell you about it while we show you the house?" Jupiter said. "Just the highlights."

Pete pointed out the window. "That's the sundial garden," he said.

"The sundial garden?" asked Mallory.

"We'll tell you about that, too," Jupiter said, turning to lead the way downstairs, while Mallory and the others followed. She loved everything they showed her about the house and thought the library one of the greatest rooms she'd ever seen in her life. In fact, she suggested that they sit in it while they finished getting caught up.

Bob and Pete and Jupiter told her that, as far as they could tell, there were actually only 51 rooms and 345 panes of glass in Castello Serreno, and though Mallory agreed when they said that the 51 rooms suggested a hidden room somewhere, she also pointed out that when it came to the nineteen missing panes of glass, it would be almost impossible for them to be in the hidden room.

"I'm not sure I agree with you," said Jupiter. "Although any windows in the hidden room would, by definition, not let in any light, there might still be panes of glass in them. Setting that aside for the moment, I'd like to return to your discovery that an ancestor of Donati and Morreti migrated to northern Italy from Bavaria not long after the Illuminati were founded."

"Andreas Ritter, who changed his name to Cavaliere," Mallory said, nodding.

"You think that his beliefs may have been passed down through the generations?" Jupiter asked.

"It seems a workable hypothesis," Mallory said. "But all the links on the genealogical site lead to Italian public records or Italian web pages. And I don't speak Italian."

"And neither do we," said Bob.

"But you told me last night on the phone that this stonemason, Clemente DeLuca, does," Mallory said to Bob. "Maybe he would help us."

"I don't know," Pete said. "I don't trust him. What if we run into information about the treasure and he doesn't tell us?"

"That, of course, is a possibility," Jupiter agreed. "Why don't we finish showing Mallory the house and then take her to meet Clemente DeLuca?"

He turned to Mallory. "Pete was suspicious of the man from the moment we met him, but although he likes to tell amazing tales, I can't quite convince myself that his friendly face conceals sinister designs. Although he did tell Ski..." As he said this, Jupiter suddenly stopped dead.

"Oh, no!" Pete almost shouted. "We forgot to tell Mallory about Skinny showing up!"

"Skinny showed up here?" Mallory asked incredulously.

"It's my fault," Pete said gloomily. "I let it slip about the treasure and where we were going. Skinny thought he might be able to find it first. He's got a friend with a camper, and he's staying in a nearby campground. This morning he cornered Mr. DeLuca and told him that he and his friend were the Two Investigators."

Mallory laughed. "Such imagination," she said.

"I wouldn't worry about it," Jupiter said. "I don't think he'll get in our way. After all, we're professionals and he doesn't know what he's doing. But it *is* annoying that he's calling himself and his friend the Two Investigators."

Mallory snorted. "I hope if he comes back to Castello Serrano while we're here, someone hits him with a rock." She didn't really mean that, but it helped her to say it aloud. "I guess we should finish the tour. Or maybe I can do that after you've left for the day."

"That's a good idea," Jupiter said. "We've only got an hour and a half left before we have to start back to the monastery for dinner."

Since Mallory had her computer bag with her, she now checked to make certain she could access the hotel's Wi-Fi, and when she found that she could, she slung the bag over her shoulder, hoping the signal would extend some distance from the house. The sun was starting to descend toward the horizon as Jupiter led the way to the garden in which three men were working on repairing stone. Immediately, one of the men came over to them. He was bald, with gold chains around his neck, and wearing a sleeveless t-shirt.

"Signorina," he said, taking one of Mallory's hands. "Che bello. Your hair is like the sun."

Though Mallory generally disliked compliments about her appearance, she found herself charmed. Clemente DeLuca, she could see, was not only a stonemason extraordinaire but also a man who loved to talk. He was gregarious and voluble, and from the moment she saw him, Mallory felt that his embellishments and fabrications were harmless – as natural to him as breathing. She was sure that Pete was wrong to suspect him of dark designs, and she explained to him what she had in mind.

"You want my help with the beautiful language of Italy?" DeLuca asked. "I am happy to give it to you. But let us go somewhere where there is shade."

They found a grove of live oaks, with chairs and a table set beneath them, and they settled themselves there. As it turned out, the hotel's Wi-Fi did extend beyond the building, and though the signal was weak, Mallory was able to get back to where she'd been the day before. She could show Bob, Pete, Jupiter, and

Clemente DeLuca what she'd found.

DeLuca's translation was halting, but as they moved through various websites, Mallory became more and more excited. A family website of one of Andreas Ritter's descendants included a history, and from it they found that Ritter had not been alone.

It seemed that three members of the Bavarian Illuminati had moved to Italy together – to Pisa, where Galileo had been born – and there had always been family rumors that they had formed a splinter sect of the original Illuminati. Its members had consisted, down through the years, of the original three extended families and their descendants.

"The Illuminati!" DeLuca said. "They were enemies of God!"

But as he kept translating, he discovered something of even more interest to him. The splinter sect had apparently collected, over the years, an incredible treasure of some kind.

"There it is!" Pete said. "I knew it."

"So it is not pirate gold," DeLuca said. "That is too bad."

The rumor was that the treasure was somehow connected to the house of Medici, a hugely rich family of bankers whose wealth and influence gave them wide political and religious influence.

"The Medici," DeLuca said reverently. "If this treasure you seek is Medici treasure — well — " He looked up into the sky as though angels would soon descend.

Mallory quickly did some additional research. "Listen to this!" she said triumphantly. "The Medici helped sponsor Galileo! He tutored Cosimo di Medici and also his mother — though she seemed to think Galileo was an astrologer. He dedicated a book about astronomy to Cosimo — who appointed him philosopher and mathematician to his father Ferdinando, the grand duke. Galileo even called the moons of Jupiter he discovered the Medicean Stars!"

"So there's every reason to think the treasure is connected to the Illuminati, to the House of Medici, and to Galileo! All three!" Jupiter said.

"Maybe you will still find the treasure in the sundial garden," DeLuca said.

"What's that?" Mallory asked. "Pete mentioned it before, but you haven't explained it."

"A garden with seven sundials," Jupiter said. "But it almost certainly doesn't have any treasure in it — other than the sundials themselves. The largest one is partly covered by a vine Mrs. Serreno told us we can clear off if we want. Since we've got to get back to the monastery for dinner at 6:00, we'll have to wait until tomorrow to do that." He turned to Clemente DeLuca. "Thank you very much, Mr. DeLuca. You've been a big help."

DeLuca smiled. "I am glad to be of service to the young Americans. Remember I cannot help you tomorrow because I go to pick up stone with il signore and la signora. We will be gone all day."

"So the hotel will be empty?" Mallory said.

"Except for Oliver Price − and Phillipa Paxton, I guess," said Jupiter.

"I hope you find the stone you need," Mallory said to DeLuca.

"Gracie, signorina." He smiled and nodded his head at her. "Addio." And he was gone.

As the four of them walked back to where the boys had stowed their bikes, they were happy to see Phillipa Paxton sitting on the porch. She'd gotten a phone call just at the end of lunch and had vanished into her room to take it. Now she told them that the call had been from the head of the History Department at her college; he was interviewing for a one-year replacement position and he wanted Phillipa to participate.

"The interview's tomorrow," she said, "so I'll be gone at least for the day. What are you guys planning to do tomorrow?"

"We're hoping to get permission to research in the monastery's archives," said Jupiter. "And we want Mallory to come and join us. But since she doesn't have her bike here, I'm not sure how she can get up the mountain."

"I can walk," Mallory said.

"Nonsense," said Phillipa. "I'll give you a ride."

"Would you really?" asked Mallory.

"I'll take you up first thing in the morning."

Mallory was sorry to see the boys bike away. It seemed like she'd only just seen them again, and even though she liked Phillipa a lot, she felt a little lost by herself.

She spent the time until dinner exploring Castello Serreno. It was a marvelous place, really, full of wonderful nooks and crannies, and the longer she was there, the more convinced she was that both Alessandro Moretti and Guisipe Donati had been extraordinary men. Men who wanted to make order out of chaos, and beauty out of ordinary forms.

But while Mallory liked all the rooms – the public rooms particularly – when she finally entered the conservatory, she was really blown away.

The elegant and carefully fitted bare stone floor, in which there were seven round flagstones, arranged in a perfect circle, the decorative and filigreed plant stands, the vaulted ceiling with the square flat section in the very middle of which was a large round skylight, the low stone wall that formed a circle under the skylight, and, maybe most of all, the elaborate instrument carved of wood which sat in the center of the circle and directly under the center of the skylight – not only was each of them impressive on its own, but together they formed a very suggestive whole – though what, exactly, they were suggesting, Mallory couldn't quite say.

The large wooden instrument under the skylight was in the form of an astrolabe, and directly above it was a window made up of twelve oblong panes of glass. Pete had been right when he'd said that the window looked like a gigantic flower with twelve glass petals – petals that were wider at the outer ends and tapered toward where they were clustered around a circular pane at the center.

As she stared upwards, Mallory was struck by the fact that not only was each individual petal of glass held securely in a leaded housing, but that there seemed to be a second level of leading underneath the top one. Although she stood on tiptoe to try to see just how that second level was constructed, the ceiling was too high above her head for her to manage it – and when she heard Fortunata Serreno ring the dinner bell, she had to abandon her exploration and head for the dining room.

At dinner, Phillipa Paxton asked her if she wanted to spend some time with her in the library after the meal, and after she and Phillipa had helped Mrs. Serreno clean up, the two of them went off together for a couple of hours of excellent conversation. Mallory felt more and more convinced that she and Phillipa might actually end up friends.

At length, however, she said goodnight. Exhausted from the travel and the excitement of the day, she climbed the spiral stairs to the Tower Room, got into bed just as it was getting dark, and was soon fast asleep.

Hours later, she woke with a start. She

glanced at her watch − it was almost 2:00 a.m., and there was a noise outside. The moon was near full, and when she looked out the window she saw, in the area of the sundial garden, what seemed to be two dark figures and darting beams of light. She knew in a flash it must be Skinny and his friend trying to find the treasure. What a total idiot Skinny was! she thought.

Mallory pulled some clothes on, grabbed the little flashlight she always took with her when she traveled, and ran down the spiral stairs and then the other stairs, and then outside. To her surprise, she didn't need to turn her flashlight on; everything was frosted by the pale light of the moon. She seethed with resentment as she dashed across the grounds toward where she had seen the two figures. When she reached the entrance to the garden, it suddenly struck her that someone other than her wretched cousin might be snooping around, and she reached out to pick up a rock from one of the flower beds in case she needed to defend herself.

As she did, she remembered saying that she hoped that if Skinny came back to Castello Serrano while she was there, someone would hit him with a rock. Still, if this *was* him, she would need to be sure she *didn't* hit him – and in another minute she was close enough to see that Skinny had, in fact, taken DeLuca's bait. He was shining a flashlight at the base of a round stone slab where his friend was digging with a shovel. Mallory carefully set the rock back on the ground, then crept as close as she could without being seen.

Skinny and his friend were talking in urgent whispers and didn't expect a thing.

"Put your hands up where I can see them," Mallory barked. "And don't move." She shone her flashlight full on Skinny's face.

"Gak!" Skinny said. He dropped his flashlight, threw his hands toward his Adam's apple, and fell over backwards. He squirmed like a bug on the ground. Though Mallory was very angry, she couldn't help laughing.

"Don't shoot!" Skinny's friend screamed. He flung the shovel aside and thrust his hands in the air. "We didn't do anything."

"It looks like you did," Mallory said. "It looks like you damaged a beautiful garden."

"Mally-Wally," Skinny said weakly. "Is that you?"

"How many times do I have to tell you my name is Mallory," she said. "Now get out of here before I decide to call the police. But first, fill in that hole you were digging and be neat about it."

"Make me," Skinny snarled as he scrambled to his feet. "I can dig a hole if I want to."

"That's perfect," Mallory said. "All your life you've been digging a hole for yourself. Now scram."

But Skinny was still so frightened from being startled that his knees buckled and he fell sideways into the hole his friend had been digging. He collapsed across the stone slab that had what Mallory could now clearly see was a gnomon in the middle.

"Ouch!" he screamed as he hit the sharp metal protrusion. As he tried to scramble to his feet, he grabbed the thick vines that covered the middle of the sundial and ripped them off, revealing something that glinted brightly in the moonlight.

"Come on, Skinny," his friend said. "Let's go." He picked up the shovel.

"I'll see you back in Rocky Beach," Skinny growled to Mallory. "And you won't see me coming."

"Oooh," Mallory said. "I'm so scared."

Skinny and his friend hurried off through the night and Mallory watched them until she couldn't see them any more. She tried to kick the dirt back into the hole that Skinny's friend had been digging, but as she did, her eye was caught again by the glint of light on what suddenly looked to her like glass. As she pulled out her flashlight, her breath caught in her throat when she found herself looking at twelve petal-shaped pieces of glass set into the plate.

Just like the petals in the skylight in the roof of the conservatory, these petals were wider at one end than at the other – the oblong ends set around what appeared to be a sun, while their tapered ends pointed toward the Roman numbers that marked the hours evenly spaced around the circle's circumference. But though Mallory could see in a flash that the petals were the same size and shape and even thickness as the petals in the conservatory's roof, she needed to point her flashlight directly on the petals' outside edges in order to see that they weren't held securely – that with some cleaning and some labor, they could be slipped out of the leading that housed them.

When she saw this, Mallory understood at once that if someone *did* slip these petals out of their current housing, they would fit perfectly into the second level of leading underneath the first one in the conservatory. Although, at the moment – and at 2:30 in the morning! – she couldn't imagine why anyone would want to do that, she felt certain she'd just discovered at least 12 of the missing 19 panes of glass.

She was so excited by the discovery that as she finished the job of kicking the dirt back into the hole Skinny and his friend had dug, she wished she could call Bob and let him know about it right away. Since she really couldn't justify waking him in the middle of the night, she contented herself with wondering what she and the others might find in the monastery's archives in the morning.

12

Trapped in The Tower Room!

Unfortunately, when Bob and the others had gotten back to the Mountain Monastery after saying goodbye to Mallory, Brother Colin had told Jupiter that the abbott's return from San Francisco had been delayed – and that unless he got back before lights out, The Three Investigators wouldn't be able to visit the archives in the morning, after all.

Bob had been disappointed to hear this – but not *too* disappointed. At least Mallory had finally arrived in the Napa Valley, and since the Serrenos, Clemente DeLuca, and Phillipa Paxton were all taking off for the day, if he, Jupiter, and Pete biked down to join her at Castello Serreno, the four of them would have the place almost to themselves.

This morning, it was porridge again in the refectory, and Bob was beginning to long for a helping of his father's blueberry pancakes – or even just a bowl of Grape Nuts or corn flakes. He was also beginning to long for a somewhat more comfortable bed – not to mention that he was tired of feeling nervous every time he got on the monastery's Wi-Fi using the day's secret password – and when Brother Colin confirmed that the archives were off for today, he began to look forward to spending the day at the castle, trying to figure out what was hidden there, and where it might be located.

At breakfast, they were once again eating in a mainly deserted refectory, but the night before, they had eaten with Brothers Anselm, Gerald, and Anders again, and now they were reviewing the conversation from that dinner.

Jupiter said, "Did Brother Anders seem different to you last evening? I thought he was more animated – or maybe more nervous – than he usually is."

"I thought so, too," Pete agreed. "He got all excited when Brother Gerald suggested taking some peas and string beans down to Castello Serreno today. Brother Anders was really eager to convince him they should wait a day or two."

"Of course," said Bob "since Fortunata is going to be gone, that was actually a good piece of advice. Still, I know what you mean. There was something strange about Brother Anders."

They finished eating, and as they left the refectory, Bob said, "We should call Phillipa and tell her that she doesn't need to bring Mallory up here, after all."

"Yes," Jupiter said. "Ask her to tell Mallory that we'll just bike down to the castle and meet her there."

When he got back to his room, Bob called Phillipa and explained the change in plans, then suggested to Jupiter and Pete that the three of them find a place outside where he could log onto the monastery's Wi-Fi and do a bit of research before leaving for Castello Serreno.

He didn't want to do it in his room because one of the brothers cleaned the guest house every morning, so he suggested walking up to the observatory and doing it there. After checking the beginning of last night's prayer, he thrust his computer into his backpack and the three of them hiked up to the observatory. The morning sun washed everything with golden light, and although there was no one around who could have seen him, even here Bob felt a little funny about pulling out his computer. Luckily, the Wi-Fi signal was still strong enough.

"What are you researching, Bob?" Jupiter asked.

"I want to look up Brother Anders," said

Bob. "And not just because he seemed nervous last night. Remember what Fortunata said about a third monk showing up at Castello Serreno one day with Brother Gerald? I think it must have been Brother Anders, and she said that he'd seemed very interested in Castello Serreno. So much so that she might have thought he was another architectural historian if she didn't know better. That struck me as odd. Although at the time there was so much going on that I didn't mention it."

"It struck me as odd, too," Jupiter said. "You wouldn't think an ex-hedge fund manager would be all that interested in buildings. And when we first met him, he seemed very reticent when I asked him about his background. He just said that he had spent the last five years in Sacramento, and that before that he had lived in San Francisco."

By now, Bob was already plugging the name "Anders Bergmann" and the words "San Francisco hedge fund" into the box on his search engine. It took a bit of fiddling with the spelling, but in very short order, Bob had landed on a now-defunct hedge fund that had been established in San Francisco under the name "The Illuminati Fund" − and which had gone out of business when its founder had been caught embezzling his clients' money!

When he reported this to Pete and Jupiter, Pete said "Holy moly!" so loudly that Bob was afraid his voice would carry all the way to the monastery – but Pete said it again, even louder, when Bob added that, stripped of his wealth, Anders Bergmann had been sent to a minimum security prison in Sacramento.

Pete almost shouted "In Sacramento! Do you think the monks knew he was a crook when they took him in?"

"They must have," Jupiter said. "They probably actually liked the fact that before his conversion, he'd been a money man."

"Just like the Pharisees Jesus threw out of the temple," Bob agreed. He'd just found a link to an article about Anders Bergmann's prison-yard conversion to Catholicism.

As Pete continued exclaiming in a combination of joy and amazement, Bob said, rather tensely, "Shhh! I want to read this!"

He did. Then he said, "Some reporter got hold of the story of this hedge-fund embezzler who got out of prison and became a monk. He went to the Mountain Monastery and interviewed some of the brothers – though not Anders Bergmann himself.

"The gist of Bergmann's story is that

one day, not long before he was due to be released, he was in the prison's exercise yard on a cloudy day in March when the clouds opened and a ray of sunlight struck him, and he heard the voice of God. Some brother or other told the reporter that when this happened, Bergmann had been the exact same age as Jesus at his crucifixion, and some other brother had compared his conversion to Saint Peter's on the road to Damascus."

"The brothers seem to have been trying hard to believe in something very unlikely," Jupiter said. "What seems much more likely is that the man now known as Brother Anders is actually the same man he always was – a thief, a criminal, and a crook."

"I agree," said Bob. "A crook who named his hedge fund after a Bavarian secret society which seems to have a strong connection to the monastery he ended up joining after he was released from prison!"

From where they sat on the steps of the observatory, Bob and his friends could see the switchbacked road leading from the valley floor to the Mountain Monastery and, just as he spoke, Bob looked up to see that, on the switchback immediately below them, a dark-colored sedan had pulled over to the side of the road. The driver didn't get out, but after a minute a figure wearing the robes of a monk emerged from a grove of what appeared to be live oaks, and bundling his robes about him, opened the door on the passenger side of the car and climbed in.

Seeing Bob's eyes locked on the road below him, Pete and Jupiter started watching the strange event, too. "What kind of car is that?" Jupiter asked Pete.

"Looks like a Camry," Pete said. "I thought monks weren't allowed to leave the monastery, except on special monastery business."

"They aren't," said Jupiter. "And I seem to remember that Mr. Price has a Camry. A blue one."

"There are lots of Camrys in California," Pete said, "and I really couldn't tell what color that one was. The sun is too bright. But what are we waiting for? We'd better get our bikes!"

Soon Bob and the others were zooming down the switchbacks of the mountain road, hoping against hope that they'd be able to catch up with the car that had picked up a renegade monk.

They didn't see the car again, but as

Bob pedaled furiously — turning and braking as needed — he found himself thinking that if Anders Bergmann and Mr. Price were in cahoots, this might be the day they planned to make their move.

Of course, it remained to be seen *what* move, precisely, but as The Three Investigators turned onto Castello Serreno's gravel driveway, Bob was disappointed to see that Oliver Price's dark blue Camry was in the spot he always parked it, and if anyone had asked Bob, he'd have said it didn't look like it had been moved.

"I guess we were wrong," Bob said ruefully.

Pete got off his bike, went over to the car, and touched the exhaust pipe. "It's hot," he said. "Somebody went somewhere."

"Interesting," Jupiter said, pinching his lip. "Let's go find Mallory."

The three of them headed for the porch and were surprised to see Oliver Price in the foyer, as if he'd been waiting for them.

"Hello, you three," Price said. "This is a surprise. I thought you were spending the day up at the monastery."

"That was our plan," Jupiter said. "We were going to do some research in the archives, but the abbot still isn't back from his trip, and we can't get in without his permission."

"So we thought we'd come back down here and look around some more," Pete said. "We're sure we're missing something."

Just then, Bob heard footsteps clattering on the stairs, and Mallory joined them, slightly out of breath.

"Boy, am I glad to see you!" she said. "You're not going to believe what happened last night – and what happened afterwards. Let's go somewhere quiet and talk."

"Roger that," said Pete. "Like where?"

"Follow me," Mallory said, turning and clattering back up the stairs. Soon she was leading them along the corridor that led to the tower room she was staying in. Bob had seen the room only briefly the day before, when he and the others had accompanied Mallory to her room. He'd seen it even more briefly when they were rushing to finish counting the rooms and the panes of glass before Mallory arrived.

But now, as the four of them pushed open the door, Bob noticed that the room's renovation still wasn't quite finished; when he grabbed the door to close it, the doorknob wobbled in his hand. In fact, it almost fell off, though Bob closed the door carefully behind him. He looked around to see a very nice room

– one with twin beds and a view of the sundial garden in the distance. There were also two small chairs set in front of the curving wall of the tower.

"Sit down," Mallory said excitedly, settling herself on the floor near one of the chairs. "I think we've had a breakthrough." Quickly, she told them about waking up the night before, discovering Skinny Norris and scaring him off – but not before he ripped the vine off the biggest sundial.

"After he left, I shone my flashlight across the stone," she said. "I found a leaded housing holding twelve glass flower petals just like the ones in the middle of the conservatory ceiling! I think they must be twelve of the nineteen missing panes of glass! Which would bring the number in the house up to 358!"

Bob had been listening to the last part of this explanation with less than his full attention, since even the mention of Skinny in the sundial garden had made him see red. Was there nothing that human pest didn't have the gall to do? Bob thought that Mallory simply running out in the night to confront him had been very brave. After all, she really couldn't have been sure until she got there that the people in the garden weren't actual burglars, or some other kind of criminal.

As for what Mallory had discovered about the extra set of flower petals, although it was interesting, Bob wasn't sure what it actually signified. After all, the point of the counting was to see if there was evidence – in numerical absence – of a hidden room.

Pete apparently shared Bob's thought. "That's really cool," he said, "but I don't see how that gets us any closer to finding the treasure."

"I know what you mean," Mallory said. "But somehow it *has* to – and I'm hoping Jupiter will be able to figure out how! It seems to me that the question is really about the skylight. I studied it after you left yesterday, and I kept wondering why Moretti designed it the way he did, rather than as a simple window. I could see that the lead housing that held the petals was really thick and complicated – and last night, after Skinny's accident, I found out why! Because if you pulled the petals out of the sundial, you could slip them into the second layer of leaded housing in the skylight!"

Jupiter was sitting in one of the two chairs, and now he pinched his bottom lip.

"A cloak of darkness," he said, almost to himself.

"What did you say?" Mallory asked.

"I was just quoting from one of the letters the architect wrote to the monk, the ones we decoded," Jupiter said. "He said something about a cloak of darkness that could be taken off, or something, to let the sun in."

"What else did the letters say?" Mallory asked.

"Moretti said that the place he'd hidden the items – or the instruments – wasn't on his blueprints," Bob said.

"That's not quite right," Jupiter said. "If I'm remembering correctly, he said that nobody would be able to guess where they were hidden from looking at his blueprints. So if he indicated where they were, he did so in a manner that would make sense only to him."

Jupiter now closed his eyes as if to remember better, and as he did, Bob said, "Of course, Mallory told us that the word Illuminati meant 'the enlightened ones', in Latin."

"That's right," Mallory said.

"The enlightened ones are the ones who have seen the light," Jupiter said. "And Moretti, in his letter, specifically mentioned the light of the sun. Remember that even if Galileo's understanding of the universe began with his discovery of four of Jupiter's moons, his real contribution was his conclusion that it was the sun – and not the earth – around which everything revolved. It would make sense if the room that really lets the sun in – the conservatory – ended up being the room that holds the key."

"If the conservatory were really about providing a place for plants," Bob said, "all that elaborate stuff in the middle wouldn't really have been necessary – the wooden carving of the astrolabe with the stone wall in a circle around it."

"The thing I don't get," said Pete, "is why anyone would put two pieces of thick molded glass on top of each other. I mean, when we were there, you said that sunlight through the skylight just as it is would be too strong and hot for almost any plant. If you doubled that, you'd have something like a magnifying glass!"

Bob nodded. "And you remember those experiments in science class where we made fire by streaming sunlight through a magnifying glass? Guiseppi Donati was terrified of fire! His house in Italy burned to the ground! Why would he have allowed anything like that?"

"True," Jupiter said. "But the second layer of glass was never installed in the housing. It just remained a possibility. But hypothetically, if the second set of glass petals was put into place, the sunlight would be concentrated on the wooden carving of the astrolabe. And wood burns. I don't think that Moretti ever intended this to happen, but if – if – "

He looked meaningfully at his friends.

"Go on!" Pete said.

"If the wooden astrolabe caught fire, burst into flame, and burned away, maybe it would reveal something underneath it."

"Like an entrance to an underground room!" Pete shouted.

Jupiter nodded. "It was there before us all the time – and we just weren't paying attention," he said. "Moretti in his letter to Brother Benedict also said that the numbers 12 and 7 would be important."

"The 12 was the twelve glass petals," Bob exclaimed with sudden certainty. "And maybe the 7 was the seven circular stones set around that stone wall under the skylight. That's the missing 19. Though that seven can't be added to the 358 for the panes of glass. After all, they're stone, not glass."

"Maybe they're both," said Jupiter intently. "Remember the part of the letter which says that light will illuminate the darkness? What if the stones in the floor are actually covering windows in the ceiling of a hidden room? My guess is that, underneath the wooden astrolabe, we'll find a mechanism that somehow opens a secret door into a secret chamber. And that when the door is opened, light will illuminate the darkness."

"So Moretti constructed an underground chamber, and he and Donati placed whatever it was down there for safekeeping," Mallory said. "If the house burned down – even to the ground – the treasure would still be safe!"

"But what *is* the treasure? What, exactly?!" Pete said.

And just as he asked this, Bob suddenly knew the answer. Not only did he know, but he knew he *had* known, in some hidden part of his mind, ever since Mallory had told them that the Medici had helped sponsor Galileo, and that Galileo had called the moons of Jupiter the Medicean Stars. The funny thing was, as Bob looked at Mallory and then at Jupiter, he could see that they were having the exact same thought.

Bob turned to Pete. "We know that three men we think were members of the Bavarian Illuminati left Bavaria at the end of the eighteenth century and moved to Italy, soon after the Illuminati were outlawed. They settled down, married Italian women, and had children."

"And they brought their beliefs with them," Jupiter added. "They founded a splinter group of the Illuminati and passed their ideas and beliefs down to their descendants. They were disciples of Galileo and his work. They thought the sun rose and set on Galileo."

"Ha ha ha," said Pete.

"About a hundred years later," Mallory said, "one of their descendants, a man named Giuseppi Donati, built a huge and expensive house in Pisa. When it burned to the ground, he went bankrupt and fled to America to make a clean start. He came to California and made a lot of money making wine."

"With some of that money, he brought his second cousin Alessandro Moretti over from Italy and asked him to design a new house," Jupiter added. "A big fancy Victorian disguised as a castle, and seemingly dedicated to astronomy and Galileo, stuffed with sundials and likenesses of telescopes and astrolabes. Bob, could you open your laptop, please, and pull up the second letter Moretti wrote to Brother Benedict? What does it say about the instruments again?"

Bob flipped open his laptop and read.

"'By then, I expect to be able to give you full details as to the housing I have devised for the Grand Geometrician's treasured instruments.'"

Jupiter nodded intently. "We thought Moretti was referring to God. But what if the Grand Geometrician doesn't refer to God, but instead – "

"To Galileo!" Pete shouted.

"And what if the treasured instruments really *are* instruments?" Jupiter asked. "Scientific instruments. Astronomical instruments. Telescopes and astrolabes – maybe made by Galileo himself."

"And if those instruments are really Galileo's – or at least date to the time of the Medici – then who knows how much they're worth?" Bob said. "A fortune, I would guess."

"Or at least of inestimable value to the world from which they have temporarily been hidden," Jupiter said.

"In this house!" Pete exclaimed excitedly.

"Under a cloak of darkness," Jupiter agreed.

They were all sitting and staring at one another in awe – but also in triumph – when they heard footsteps climbing the spiral stairs to the door. Since Oliver Price was the only other person in the house at the moment, Bob knew it must be him, and when Mallory called out, "Come in!" he saw that he was right.

"I'm sorry to bother you," Price said. "But I find that I need to run to town to pick up some supplies, and I wanted to tell you that I'll be gone for three or four hours. You'll have the place to yourselves. Enjoy it!"

Although Price's words seemed innocent enough, all of a sudden Bob found himself wondering whether maybe it really *had* been Oliver Price picking up that unidentifiable monk on the road to the Mountain Monastery, and if so, if his interest in Castello Serreno was more than just the interest of a man who wanted to write a popular history about a house with rumors of hidden treasure.

He hardly had time to think this out when Price nodded, turned, and left the room, closing the door behind him. As he did, the inside doorknob fell off and hit the floor. It was a white ceramic doorknob, but although it hit the wooden boards of the floor quite hard, it didn't crack or break.

"Oh, my," said Price from the other side. "The knob just came off in my hand! I am so sorry! Can you open the door on your side?"

"Our knob fell off, too," Pete said. "The

door swings in. Can you fix the knob out there?"

Banging noises came from the other side of the door. "It's locked!" Price said. "I don't know how that happened. But don't worry, I'll get you out somehow."

"How?" Jupiter asked.

"Before I go to town, I'll find a phone book," Price said. "There must be a locksmith in one of the towns around here. I'll find someone who can make it out to the house today."

"Today?" Pete said. "How about right now?"

"I am so sorry," Price said again. "Just be patient. Locksmiths can be busy and whoever I find may take a while to arrive. But he should be here in a couple of hours."

"A couple of hours!" Bob said, as he listened to Price descend the stairs. "Jupe, do you have your Swiss Army knife?"

"Of course," said Jupiter, reaching into his pocket and pulling it out. He used the blade of his knife and attempted to pry the door open, but it didn't budge. He tried to use the blade, and the screwdriver, and scissors to unlock the mechanism, but nothing worked – and when Pete suggested pulling the pins on the door hinges, Jupiter found that they wouldn't budge.

Bob gulped. What were they going to do? With a little luck and a lot of serious thinking, they had figured out the secret of Castello Serreno – but now they were trapped in the Tower Room and might be here for hours and hours. He couldn't help but think it was ironic that in a house built to remind its inhabitants of the inexorable – and scientifically inarguable – forward movement of time, he would be sitting here feeling as if time had stopped!

13

Jupiter Gets Discouraged

Five minutes later, Jupiter was feeling both frustrated and glum. In fact, he was feeling like an idiot. When the door of the tower room had slammed shut, he had known right away that the doorknob hadn't come off in Price's hand accidentally, and that it had indeed been Price they'd seen on the mountain road in the blue sedan.

Although it hadn't been unreasonable for Jupiter to let his suspicions be lulled by Price's open admission that he was not a real historian but just someone interested in writing a popular book about a rumored treasure, Jupiter knew he should never have ignored his own uneasy sense that there were villains about. And once Bob had discovered that Brother Anders was almost certainly a phony monk, Jupiter should have been especially on guard.

The problem was that, even now, although he had a high degree of confidence that Anders Bergmann and Oliver Price were in cahoots — that they knew about the treasure in the secret room, and that the moment they'd learned that Castello Serreno would be deserted they'd decided to make their move, Jupiter still couldn't be totally certain he was right. He might, conceivably, be putting two and two together and getting five.

And although both Bob and Mallory had their phones and could have called 911, what would they have said? *Help! We're stuck in a room! Maybe there's a robbery taking place!* The sudden arrival of a patrol car, siren blaring, didn't strike him as the best solution. Surely they could find a way out of this room, and, after all, it would be far more satisfying for the four of them to foil the would-be robbers than to have the police do it.

At the moment, Bob was explaining to Mallory about Anders Bergmann.

"But you mean the monks *knew* he was a criminal before they accepted him into their order?" she asked in amazement. "Why would they do that?"

"Because he's a good actor and tells convincing lies!" said Pete.

"Because they probably really wanted to believe he was a sinner redeemed," said Bob. "He supposedly had his come-to-Jesus moment in the exercise yard at the prison, and after that he decided to dedicate his life to prayer and contemplation in service to God."

"What a crock!" Pete said. "And what a crook!"

"A clever cover, actually," Jupiter said rather wearily. "The monks, on the whole, are quite old. Almost all of them are in their 50s, 60s, and 70s. To have a bright young man with a criminal past show up and want to join them must have given them hope and a jolt of energy."

"They won't take the news very well, I bet," Pete said.

"They have a great deal of equanimity," Jupiter said. "I expect they'll absorb the truth and go on about their business."

"So the *wunderkind* wasn't a wunderkind at all," Mallory said.

"Just a common criminal," Jupiter said, "if a clever one. And I bet Oliver Price has a criminal history, too. In fact, I wouldn't be surprised if the two of them met in prison and cooked up this whole plan there."

"But how would they even have known about it? About what was really hidden in this house?" Mallory asked.

"That's a very good question," Jupiter said. "Though at the moment, what we should really be trying to do is to figure out a way to get out of this room. I know Bob and Mallory have cellphones, but I don't want to involve Castello Serreno in a scandal before the hotel has even opened by calling the police before we know for sure what's going on."

"I think you're right, Jupe," Bob said, nodding. "It would be best to try to catch Price and Bergmann in the act of doing something bad. And we can't do that by staying locked in here."

Jupiter got to his feet and opened one of the tower's windows. He reached out as far as he could and swept his hand over the house's siding. When he pulled himself back into the room, he shook his head.

"It's only about twenty or twenty-five feet to the ground, and if this was a stone house, we might have a chance of simply climbing down. With the wood shingles, there are plenty of handholds, but the shingles would just rip off. If only we had a rope, we could fasten it around one of these central mullions and climb down it to the ground."

Pete jumped to his feet and flipped open a cupboard door – the same cupboard door that Jupiter had seen in almost every room, and that had once contained a rope. But not this time. The cupboard was empty – and so was Jupiter's head, he feared. The shot of adrenaline he'd gotten from calling himself an idiot was beginning to fade, and he felt more and more helpless and irritated.

Right now, as they sat there talking, Price and Bergmann might be opening up the secret room beneath the conservatory – planning to steal astronomical instruments from the 16th and 17th centuries, worth millions and millions of dollars, but really invaluable to the study of science and history. There was no way for Jupiter to guess how Price and Bergmann had even gotten wind of the treasure in the first place. If they had been in prison together, how would they have heard of it?

Still, either Price or Bergmann must have stumbled on information which led them to believe the treasure was real and that it remained unfound. Otherwise, the two of them would never have gone to the trouble to create such an elaborate subterfuge.

Jupiter glanced at Mallory. She was thinking hard, and as she did, a series of expressions flashed across her face – pleasure, impatience, anger, admiration. Ever since he had met her, Jupiter had been impressed with how smart Mallory was, but the longer he had known her, the more impressed he was with the range of her interests, and also with her grit.

If she hadn't been brave enough to dash out into the sundial garden the night before, Skinny's accidental unmasking of the glass petals on the sundial would never have happened, and the four of them would simply be sitting here, trapped in a room, rather than sitting here after having unraveled the essence of the puzzle. She'd been right there with Jupiter, every step of the way, matching his insights and deductions with her own.

In fact, even if Jupiter hadn't been there, she'd have arrived at the truth, he thought. Her interest in architecture, and in buildings in general, had encouraged her to study the bottom layer of lead housing in the conservatory skylight in a way that he himself hadn't really bothered to, and her amazingly precise visual memory had let her see that the housing on the sundial was identical. Jupiter was struck by the fact that he had never before seen how fascinating buildings were – they were actually three-dimensional maps of the minds that had envisioned them and then created them.

As he sat there wondering what to do next, he also thought again about Headquarters – a building close to his heart. When Bob and Pete had first suggested that it was time to replace it with something else, he'd resisted the suggestion, but he knew it was true that it had gotten too small for them – and shabby as well – and that it was time to expand their base of operations. Time to let the sun in.

After all, The Three Investigators were established now, and older than they had been when it had thrilled them to know that their Headquarters was a secret. They had a website and a growing reputation. They could use a bigger and better Headquarters – one that was more adult, and that clients could enter to have consultations – and with Mallory's ability and love of buildings, it would be great if she would design it, Jupiter thought.

However, now was not the time to propose it. They had to find a way to get out of the tower room and back in the world at large. But how could they do that without a rope? He'd been thinking of other things so deeply that he was surprised to hear that Mallory, Bob, and Pete had already come up with a solution.

"Well, no," Mallory was saying. "I've never done it. Or seen it done. But I've read about it in a *lot* of novels. English novels, mostly. In English novels, people are *always* knotting sheets together, tying them around the mullions of window, then climbing to the ground."

"How many sheets does it take?" asked Pete.

"I don't know," Mallory said. "But there are two beds in this room, and I would think that four sheets would be plenty."

Jupiter did a quick mental calculation – a sheet for an extra-long twin bed must be about a hundred inches long, and if they knotted four of them them together, then added knots every five or six feet, they should have at least twenty-five feet of sheet – though tying part of that around the mullion would make the total length less. Still, even if they had to drop a couple of feet to the ground at the end, the plan should work.

"That's a great idea, Mallory," he said. "Let's do it." He and Mallory jumped to their feet and while Mallory headed to one bed, he headed to the other. Bob joined Mallory and Pete joined him, and in very short order they had stripped the beds of their other coverings and were tying and knotting a single long sheet-rope. After throwing open the two adjacent windows, they tied the end of the rope around the thick wooden mullion between them, then dropped the rope toward the ground. Its end came within a safe and easy couple of feet.

"It's going to work!" said Pete. "I'll go first. Now that Jupe's getting skinnier all the time, I'm the heaviest of all of us, and if the sheets hold me, they'll hold everyone."

"That's true," Jupiter said. "But Bob and Mallory have a lot more experience at climbing than you and I do. Not this kind of climbing, granted."

"No," said Bob. "We can't rappel down a rope like this one. We'll just have to grip the top knots with our hands, and use the bottom knots to support our feet. Even so, I think I should go first, then Mallory. You and Pete can watch what we do and do the same thing afterwards. I'm pretty sure the rope will be strong enough for all of us."

Without pausing for an answer, Bob climbed onto one of the chairs, grabbed the rope, hoisted himself over the sill, and began descending. He moved gracefully and easily from one knot to the next. Jupiter was impressed. Bob waved when he hit the ground, and Mallory clambered up on the sill, then down the rope. Pete followed, and with his three friends safely on the ground, it was Jupiter's turn.

He was a bit apprehensive, as he always

was with a physical activity he was trying for the first time, especially one like this, with its inherent dangers. He also didn't much like heights. He thought for a moment that maybe he didn't need to go down — that one of his friends could come up and let him out. But then he remembered the door was locked both ways, and wasn't opening anytime soon. And besides, he could do this!

He got on his knees on the windowsill, holding tight to the rope, and then started descending. Before he knew it, he was almost down. He hit the ground harder than he'd expected, but he was there. It had been at least a half an hour since Oliver Price had locked them in the tower room, and although that wasn't enough time for him and his partner to have opened up the secret room beneath the conservatory and made off with the treasure, it was time enough for them to have gotten started.

Indeed, when Jupiter had O.K.'d the plan to escape from the tower room, he'd been counting on Anders Bergmann and Oliver Price being inside the castle, too engrossed in their criminal activities to notice that the chickens they thought securely locked away had flown the coop.

But now it was vital that the four of them get under cover, somewhere in the house, fast, and gesturing to the others to follow him, Jupiter sprinted around the corner to the back, where one of the twelve exterior doors led to the kitchen. The kitchen was as far away from the conservatory as any room in the house, and any noise they made there wouldn't be heard by the crooks.

In short order, the four of them were hiding in one of the little pantries built into the larger butler's pantry, talking softly.

"Maybe we should just call the police now," Mallory said. "Although you're right that it would be best to try to catch Price and Bergmann in the act, how are we going to do that? If we get close enough to see them, they'll be able to see *us*."

"And even though there are only two of them, they're bigger and stronger than we are," added Bob. "And if they know they've been found out, they may be desperate."

"No!" Pete said. "We can do this. Do you think they're more dangerous than Slade De Marco and Russell Tate?"

They were the men who had kidnapped Pete and Bob the previous summer.

"No," Bob said. "But – "

"Besides," Pete said. "That would take all the fun out of this. Don't you want to be able to tell Felix and Fortunata about the treasure we've found in their house? After we've found it ourselves? Besides, if we called the police, there's a good chance that Oliver Price could talk his way out of this. He hasn't committed any crime yet."

"That's right," Jupiter said. "He could just tell the police he'd inadvertently discovered the house's secret and wanted to surprise Mr. and Mrs. Serrano when they got back from their stone-buying expedition. He could also tell them that the story would be a great one for his so-called book."

Bob sighed. "That makes a lot of sense. So I guess it's up to us."

"What I'm wondering about," said Jupiter, "is how exactly they plan to get the secret room opened up. Even if they know about the twelve petals in the sundial, I can hardly imagine they're going to insert them in the skylight and wait around for the wooden astrolabe to burst into flame. Sun through a magnifying glass can reach a temperature close to 400 degrees Fahrenheit, but there's all that space between the skylight and the wood. Even if those panes up there magnify the sunlight, it would take a while for the plan to work."

"How hot does it need to be to burn wood?" Mallory asked.

"Just under 600 degrees Fahrenheit," Jupiter said. "I think. But if the lens was doubled – no problem. The wood would burn, eventually. Not right away, though. And anyway, their whole plan clearly hinges on no one ever discovering the theft. They must be assuming – as I am – that there's a way to get the wooden housing off and expose the mechanism for opening the room without actually burning the housing. As we know, Giuseppe Donati was terrified of fire. I sincerely doubt that either he or his architect truly imagined that the astrolabe would ever burn."

He squinted and pinched his bottom lip.

"We have to remember that Moretti was working in the realm of symbol," Jupiter went on. "When he wrote of light illuminating the darkness in his letters to Brother Benedict, he not only meant letting light into the hidden room, but also letting the fire of human reason burn away superstition, emotion, and false belief. Like Galileo did.

"I wish I'd looked more closely at the astrolabe," he added. "I bet there are wooden pegs or something similar concealed in the decorative base. After all, Guiseppe Donati would have wanted to have regular access to his secret room. There's not much point in owning a lot of priceless and fascinating scientific instruments if you can't see them whenever you want to.

"Maybe before he even arrived, Oliver Price bought a handheld device that let him walk all over the house and the grounds, using ground-penetrating radar. I've read about it. It sends an electromagnetic pulse into the floor or the wall or the ground. The pulse hits something hard and bounces back to a receiver. The speed and the strength of the pulse's return gives you information about the density of the space it has traveled through."

"Maybe," Bob said. "That could be how he found it. But it had to be after we saw him on his hands and knees measuring the floor of his room. Though, you know, Jupe," he added, seeming to reconsider. "If we could figure out the secret without GPR, so could they. I'm betting Anders Bergmann read the original of the letters to Brother Benedict."

"That's true," Jupiter said. "But either way, what we want is to catch them in the act of opening the room up. We're no closer to doing that sitting in this pantry than we were

267

locked in the tower room."

"Why don't we go into the secret passage between the library and the drawing room?" Mallory asked. "I went through it last night after you left, and where it opens into the drawing room, you can see into the conservatory pretty clearly. We could hide behind the tapestry and see if the two of them are there."

"I can have my phone in my hand," Bob added. "And the minute we see what they're doing, we can go back up the passage and call the police. At the moment, Price thinks we're still safely locked away. Though he knows we know about the rumor of the treasure. He must have been freaked when we showed up."

"And Bergmann probably suspected something too," Jupiter said. "Still, I think Mallory's idea is excellent." He got to his feet and quietly and cautiously led the way to the library. There, he was about to pull the lever that opened the door to the secret passage when Pete saw the copper stand next to the ornate fireplace that held the fireplace tools – a number of pokers, a set of heavy wrought iron tongs.

"Hey," Pete said. "I've got an idea. If we need something to threaten the crooks with, we could use those iron pokers."

"Good thinking, Second!" Jupiter said. Pete grabbed the pokers, and Jupiter pulled the lever opening the door of books.

It was dim in the passageway, even with the door open, but still, the first thing Jupiter noticed was a piece of paper lying on the floor. He picked it up and saw that it was a copy of the Mountain Monastery prayer from the night before; in the right hand corner were the words "Brother Anders," and on the back was a list of numerical notations – which appeared, from what Jupiter could see, to be phone numbers.

"We were right about Brother Anders!" said Pete. "And that's the prayer we got last night! But what's it doing here?"

"My guess," Jupiter said, "is that when we surprised Price and Bergmann by coming back here unexpectedly, they panicked. If we had actually seen Bergmann, it would have raised a lot of questions they didn't want to answer. So when we arrived, Price greeted us, but Bergmann hid in here. He must have dropped the prayer with the phone numbers on the back by accident. Let's go see if they're in the conservatory." He led the way to the other end of the passage.

There, he gestured to the others to keep back, and when he touched the hidden lever, the door slid sideways into the wall. Very carefully, Jupiter pushed the fabric out an inch or two, and, peering through the tiny slit, he saw that there were indeed two men in the conservatory. But while one of them was clearly Anders Bergmann – no longer wearing his monk's robe – the other man didn't look like Oliver Price.

In fact, if his eyes were not deceiving him, the other man looked a lot like one of Clemente DeLuca's Italian assistants! Not Lorenzo Costa – the tall one who had had a foolish grin on his face every time Jupiter had seen him – but Umberto Mancini, the heavy-set and heavy-bearded man with a thick mustache and jet-black hair.

Behind Jupiter, Pete and Mallory were whispering together, but although he knew they must be eager to be filled in on what was going on in the conservatory, he waved his hand to quiet them and kept watching. Jupiter was almost certain it was Mancini who was kneeling inside the stone circle fiddling at the base of the astrolabe. But as he leaned forward to see a bit more clearly, there was a loud noise behind him in the passage. Jupiter dropped the tapestry in alarm as he turned to see that Pete had lost hold of one of the pokers, which had clattered loudly to the floor.

"Oh, no!" Pete said, almost as loudly, picking it up. Jupiter quickly slid the door back across the end of the passage and gestured to the others to run toward the other end and get back through the entrance into the library. What a mess they were making of this investigation!

14

Pete Takes Charge

When Pete saw Jupiter's gesture, he didn't need to be told twice. What a klutz he could be sometimes! He'd been holding the poker so carefully, and now he'd gone and dropped it. He turned and bolted, followed by his three friends.

Instinctively – although at a run this time – Pete started retracing his path through the house which had brought the four of them from the kitchen to the secret passage. In very short order, they were back in the tiny pantry. Once there, they closed the door and tried to still their breathing as they listened for pursuing footsteps – and when they couldn't hear any, they all breathed a little more quietly.

"So what did you see, Jupe?" asked Pete as soon as he could get the words out. "I'm sorry I dropped a poker," he added, setting both of them carefully along the wall. "That was really, really stupid."

"No, it wasn't," Mallory said. "It was just an accident. But what *did* you see?" she asked Jupiter.

"I saw two men in the conservatory — and they weren't Anders Bergmann and Oliver Price," Jupiter said grimly. "They were Anders Bergmann and Umberto Mancini. Bergmann has dropped the monk thing and is wearing street clothes."

"Umberto Mancini?" Pete said — remembering to keep his voice down but also remembering the brief private conversation he'd had with the man the day he'd met Clemente DeLuca.

Pete hadn't exactly covered himself in glory in the course of this case — so far at least! Before the case had even gotten started, he'd managed to let Skinny Norris know what they were up to; a while ago he'd managed to drop a poker just when they were finally closing in on the bad guys; and in between the first and second careless actions, he'd forgotten to share an important clue with Bob, Jupiter, and Mallory.

He almost blushed as he remembered Mancini saying "There's no treasure here," and then, when Pete asked why he was sure, saying, "Because my parents are from Pisa, and their parish priest told them that all the rumors were total nonsense. About the celestial globe that had been made by a Muslim astronomer almost a thousand years ago, and then taken to America."

Pete now told the story quickly.

"The thing is, when Mancini said that thing about a celestial globe, I knew right away there was something strange about it," Pete admitted. "But by then I had decided that Clemente DeLuca was the suspicious character, so I didn't follow up on just how suspicious it was that Mancini had a really specific story about a really specific treasure."

"Much more specific than anything Clemente DeLuca had mentioned," Jupiter said, nodding his head in agreement. "It therefore seems highly probable that the reason Mancini applied for the job of assistant stonemason to begin with was that he was already working with Anders Bergmann and Oliver Price.

"And I'm now wondering whether the reason Oliver Price took off for town this morning was to trade his Camry for a panel van of some kind – a van in which they could haul away the loot. I'm afraid that, at this point, we really have little choice but to call the authorities. Bob, do you want to do the honors?"

But just as Bob pulled his cellphone out and flipped it open, Pete heard footsteps outside the pantry, and he hardly had time to freeze in panic before the door was flung open and Anders Bergmann was leaning over to grab Bob's phone right out of his astonished hands. Behind him stood Umberto Mancini and Oliver Price.

"Hello, my young friends," Price said. "I guess I should cancel my call to the locksmith. You seem to have gotten out of the tower room all by yourselves."

As for Bergmann, he made no pretense of joviality. His expression was fierce, his face was flushed, and, with his normally pale coloring and blond hair, he looked very angry. He had made a very convincing monk and now he was a very convincing bad guy.

"I thought you were trouble from the first time I saw you," Bergmann said. "Why would three teenage boys be staying at a monastery? All right. Keep your hands where we can see them, and don't try any funny stuff. If anyone else has a cellphone, we want it now."

Mallory slipped her hand into a pocket, pulled out her cellphone, and handed it to Bergmann. He, in turn, handed both of the cellphones to Price, who − still jovially, and even humorously − tossed them into a large ceramic jar marked FLOUR which stood on a

275

shelf in the pantry. Then he stepped into the pantry and patted Pete and Jupiter down to make sure they weren't hiding cellphones of their own.

"Now get to your feet and march," said Bergmann. "We haven't got all day to finish our work, and I want you under my eyes the whole time. If you're quiet and cooperative, we *may* let you go at the end − but if you give us any trouble while we're in the underground room, you may find yourself spending some time in it. A lot of time. In fact, if you don't do exactly what we say, you can have it to your-selves for all eternity − along with the skeleton of Alessandro Moretti!"

Although Pete knew he was just saying this to scare them, the fact was, he *was* scared − scared enough so that he lunged quickly side-ways and grabbed the two pokers he had set against the wall of the pantry.

"Come on," he yelled to the others. He tossed the second poker to Jupiter. "Let's get them!"

At that, all three of the men backed away as quickly as possible, and when Jupiter, Pete, Bob, and Mallory followed them just as quickly, they all found themselves in the kitchen where Bergmann immediately grabbed a heavy iron skillet, Umberto Mancini a copper-bottomed saucepan, and Oliver Price a large kettle from a hanging rack.

"Don't fight them," Jupiter said. "We need to get out of here and find a way to call the police."

Holding his poker in front of him to fend off a sudden attack, Jupiter started backing toward the outside door, but as he did, Mancini suddenly rushed at Pete, swinging the copper-bottomed saucepan. At the final instant, he veered away and thwapped Bob on the shoulder with the pan instead.

Bob crumpled at the impact, and in an instant, Anders Bergmann had grabbed a length of clothesline from the counter and a knife from a knife rack. He slashed the rope into pieces, then tossed a length to Mancini, who grabbed Bob's wrists and tied them together.

He pulled Bob to his feet, held him in front of him, and said, "The rest of you better behave, or we're going to hurt your little friend. Now walk ahead of us, and keep your mouths shut."

By now, Bergmann had also tossed the knife to Umberto Mancini, and Mancini was holding it in a menacing manner near Bob's throat, so Pete, Jupiter, and Mallory all did exactly as he suggested – even down to the instruction to keep their mouths shut. They all trooped out of the kitchen, with Mancini shoving Bob. Pete, Jupiter, and Mallory followed, and Anders Bergmann and Oliver Price brought up the rear.

Pete knew what Bob was feeling; less than a year before, he himself had been a similarly helpless hostage when he was in the hands of the counterfeiter André Laurent. Although that had been a highly unpleasant experience, this was even more unpleasant, Pete thought, as he walked through the corridors of Castello Serreno, watching Bob's back. Somehow the blow to his shoulder had broken the skin. Bob's shirt now had a patch of blood on it.

In fact, being unable to free someone he cared about from the clutches of a ruthless criminal was really one of the worst feelings Pete had ever had, and it made the walk to the conservatory seem much longer than it really was. At last, they arrived, and Anders Bergmann ordered The Three Investigators and Mallory to sit on the floor next to the far wall. Bob was still bleeding, and his face looked dangerously white, but when Mallory said, "I think Bob should lie down," Umberto Mancini just sneered and said, "And I think he shouldn't."

He took the rest of the pieces of the rope belt and tied Jupiter, Mallory, and Pete's hands together in front of them.

While this should have made Pete feel even more helpless, he had recently learned from an action movie how to hold your wrists in a certain, clever way if someone was trying to tie them together. After Mancini was done, Pete tested the rope and felt a surge of hope. He could feel, by wriggling his wrists, that he'd managed to introduce a significant amount of slack.

However, to Pete's dismay, Mancini now picked up the knife Anders Bergmann had taken from the kitchen. Pete had been hoping he could get to the knife and cut the rope, that wasn't going to happen, after all. He sat quietly for a moment, watching the three bad guys.

While Mancini stood guard, Oliver Price and Anders Bergmann knelt in the middle of the stone circle under the flower-petal skylight, talking quietly as they examined the wooden astrolabe. From what Pete could hear, Price was explaining to Bergmann how he thought some hidden catches should work, but Bergmann was having trouble getting them to do so.

After some five minutes of this, Umberto Mancini called out, "Just break the frickin' thing with a hammer! Unless you really want to leave these four inside the room when we're done with it."

The first time the idea of leaving them in the secret room had been mentioned, Pete had felt that Bergmann had simply been trying to scare them, but when Umberto Mancini said it, Pete got the sense that he was entirely serious. He was suggesting that he and his partners would need to determine how to handle their prisoners before they could decide how to handle the wooden astrolabe and whatever lay beneath it.

Whoa! Pete thought. That was genuinely scary, and it was even scarier when Anders Bergmann glanced over to where Umberto Mancini was standing. "Yessss," he said, in a considering sort of tone. Pete glanced around, wondering what on earth they could do, and as he did, he saw, for the first time, that Jupiter had been right again.

A white van stood in the driveway – not where Price's Camry had previously been parked, but directly in front of the nearest outside door – with the rear of the van pulled up almost to the steps. The tail pipe was leaking a bit of smoke, so Pete knew the motor had been left running. It was clear that although the villains intended to simply carry the stolen goods to the van, load it up, and drive off, they were also anticipating the possibility that they might have to make a quick getaway.

Was there some way he could get to the van and slash its tires or something? At first, Pete couldn't see how he could get out of the conservatory without being caught, but then he noticed that one of the tall windows on the wall against which he and the others were sitting had been left partially open.

It wasn't a double-hung window, but a casement, the kind that cranked open outwards. Although this one wasn't open enough for him to just jump out of, he thought he might be able to kick it hard enough to break the hinges off and jump through it afterwards. Playing soccer was a lot of fun, but it also trained your legs to do things you wouldn't have imagined possible before you tried them. Yes, he thought, he could probably do it. It would break the window, of course, but that wouldn't matter to the Serrenos.

Just then, two things happened at almost exactly the same surprising moment. Anders

Bergmann, still on his knees, fumbling to free the hidden catches on the wooden astrolabe, suddenly called out, "I think I've got it!" – and down the long and winding driveway leading to Castello Serreno Pete and everyone else in the conservatory suddenly heard a car approaching.

Pete craned his neck to see that it was Mrs. Serreno's car – and when Oliver Price also saw who it was, he nodded to the others and said grimly, "I'll take care of this." As Price left the conservatory, Bergmann climbed out of the stone well in its center and joined Mancini in standing guard. He had brought one of the pokers from the kitchen with him, and now he held it in a menacing manner next to Mancini's knife.

Something about this gesture really made Pete angry. He could see Bergmann was seriously spooked. His eyes skittered from one of them to the next, and to Mancini, whose face had hardened into a mask of aggression. Before he knew what was happening, Pete was straining against the rope, chafing his wrists this way and that, struggling to get them free. And then suddenly they were! The rope fell away. In a flash, he jumped to his feet and tackled Bergmann. The poker skidded across the floor, and when Pete picked it up, he swung it at Umberto Mancini's legs.

Amazingly, he hit them very solidly. Mancini yelled in pain and alarm and staggered sideways.

"Damn you!" he screamed.

By now, Mallory, Bob, and Jupiter were all on their feet as well – although with their wrists still tied – and when he saw what was happening, Bergmann suddenly grabbed Bob around the waist and pulled him close.

"Stay away from me," Bergmann yelled, "or I'll hurt your friend again!"

"Let him go," Pete retorted, "or you're the one who'll get hurt."

Pete raised the poker again and charged. Bergmann tried to move backwards, but Bob didn't budge. Instead, he raised his left leg, bent his knee, and kicked backwards as hard as he could. He caught Bergmann's kneecap and the man howled and let go of him, falling backwards.

Bergmann was now on the stone floor writhing in pain, holding his knee.

"Watch him!" Pete yelled to Bob. "If he even tries to get up, kick him again as hard as you can."

He turned back to see that Mancini was

now jabbing with the kitchen knife – thrusting it toward Mallory and then toward Jupiter. Pete thwacked him again behind the knees with the poker, and this time, the knife flew to the floor. Jupiter, who seemed to have been waiting for this, picked it up and cut Mallory free. Quickly she took the blade and cut him and Bob loose. They were four against two now!

As Pete stood breathing hard, he looked through the wall of windows and saw that Oliver Price was standing with Fortunata who was holding Luciano by the hand. As Pete and the others watched, Price bent over and grabbed the boy.

Even if he'd been outside, Pete would have been too far away to hear what Price said to Fortunata, or what she said to him, but she screamed as her son was suddenly lifted into the air and started wailing.

A hot white rage washed over Pete.

Without pausing for another instant, Pete ran to the open window he had previously sighted, kicked it right off its metal hinges, and jumped through. He and the window crashed to the ground at almost the same instant, and as Fortunata, Luciano, and Oliver Price all looked up to see what the commotion was, Pete sprinted toward them as fast as he could.

Price turned and ran as well – with Luciano over his shoulder – and, tearing after Price and his captive, Pete suddenly saw, out of the corner of his eye, Anders Bergmann and Umberto Mancini lurch into the doorway, limping. Bergmann called out to Price, and Price turned, still clutching Luciano.

"Come on!" Bergmann called. "We've got to get out of here! Bring the kid! We'll take him as a hostage!"

Price turned and dashed toward the van, Luciano's head bobbing dangerously on his shoulder. Pete could hear Mrs. Serreno calling out – alternately trying to reassure her son and pleading with Price to put him down.

Bergmann and Mancini had made it to the van and were turning it around, its tires squealing on the gravel. Mallory, Bob, and Jupiter had now run onto the porch of the house – Jupiter holding the poker, and Bob holding the knife.

Swerving sideways, Pete grabbed the poker from Jupiter, then ran back to intercept Oliver Price. He missed catching him by a whisker, but as Price jumped into the van's open passenger-side door, still clutching his wailing hostage, Pete swung the poker and smashed the window. Mancini, who was driving, was so startled by the sudden shattering glass that he took his foot off the gas just long enough for Pete to reach into the still-open door and wrest Luciano out of Oliver Price's arms.

Luciano was still screaming, and his face was red and filled with fear, but as he felt Pete's arms around him − and as Pete ran backwards to get out of the path of the rapidly speeding-up van − he suddenly stopped crying and said, "Pit!" The van headed down the driveway as fast as Mancini could force it, leaving a spray of gravel in its wake.

Pete turned to see Fortunata running toward him. She must have been six months pregnant, but that didn't stop her, and as Pete hoisted Luciano into her waiting arms, she started crying in joy as well as relief. Pete almost felt like crying, too. But he didn't, because after an initial happy reunion with his mother, Luciano decided he was tired of being in *anyone's* arms and struggled to get down on the ground.

There, he started running toward Jupiter, Bob, and Mallory − running as fast as his chubby little legs would carry him − and when he reached them, he suddenly sat down. Somehow this made the four of them start laughing, and although Mrs. Serreno was still very shaken, she started laughing too.

It turned out that she and Luciano had come back from Sacramento almost as soon as they'd arrived. Luciano had slept badly last night and had been fussing nonstop. Since it would take hours and hours for Clemente De-Luca and Mr. Serreno to select the needed stone, she'd decided to come home again and let Luciano have a proper nap.

On their side, Pete and the others told her that when they hadn't been able to get access to the archives at the monastery, they'd come to Castello Serreno instead, and after putting their heads together while sitting in the Tower Room, they'd discovered that they really didn't need the archives after all.

Pete listened as Jupiter and Mallory filled Fortunata in on the rest of what had happened.

"We think there has to be a way to take the astrolabe off its base without damaging it," Jupiter said. "Obviously, Donati would have wanted to be able to visit his collection of scientific treasures. If we hadn't been interrupted, we would probably have tried to open the room today. As it was, the thieves beat us to it — although they didn't actually get anything open."

The longer Jupiter and Mallory talked

about what they thought they knew, the more delighted and interested Mrs. Serreno seemed.

"But if you can get into the room, you have to do it! I can't think of a better present for Felix when he gets back from Sacramento!" she said. "He has always been interested in astronomy, and if there really is a celestial globe made by a Muslim astronomer almost a thousand years ago in his very own house, he will be over the moon. Over the four moons of Jupiter, perhaps I should say! He will feel such a thing connects this house directly to the great Muslim astronomer Ibn al-Haytham – just as the astrolabe connects it to Mariam al-Astrulabe."

"Who's Mariam al-Astrulabe?" asked Mallory.

"That's right!" said Pete. "You weren't here the day the Serrenos told us about her."

"She was a Muslim astronomer, too – the one credited with the invention of the astrolabe," Jupiter explained to Mallory. He turned back to Fortunata. "It would be terrific if we can get the secret room open, but we should call the police first. Although Bergmann and Price didn't actually steal anything, they intended to, and they did try to kidnap Luciano. Attempted abduction is a crime."

"They also threatened us and tied us up," said Bob. "That's unlawful confinement."

"Not to mention assault," Mallory said. "Your poor shoulder."

Pete's mind returned to the counterfeiter, André Laurent – a man who was now once again in prison as a result of Pete's testimony against him in court. As he thought back on the experience, he felt reluctant ever to do it again.

"That's true," Pete said. "And I guess we probably *should* report what happened. Though I wish we didn't have to."

Luciano – who had been playing happily with some pebbles on the floor of the porch – looked up as if he approved of Pete's position, then climbed into Pete's lap. Pete smiled and bounced him around a bit.

"You're going to be a great father," Mrs. Serrano said. "I can tell."

This surprised Pete a lot, but it also pleased him – so much that he found himself blushing. He tried to stop it before the blush got really evident, but as usual, he couldn't do it. To change the subject as quickly as he could, he said, "Maybe. But in the meantime, I want to see what's really in the secret room. What if Bergmann was right about Alessandro

Moretti's skeleton being down there?"

"Bergmann was just saying that to frighten us," Jupiter said. "There's no skeleton down there."

"Are you sure?" Pete asked.

"Absolutely," Jupiter said. "Pete, you amaze me. You can overpower two bad guys in no time, but you're frightened by the idea of a skeleton?"

Pete smiled sheepishly, as if he really were. He wasn't − well, not really − but pretending he was was better than trying to imagine a distant future when he might be a father. Now, *that* was a scary thought, for sure!

15

Folding Back The Cloak of Darkness

Two hours later, Mallory was still reeling from the events of the morning. To have seen Bob get attacked by the mad Italian – though, as it turned out, the abrasion on his shoulder was superficial and all he'd have is a big bruise – and to have been tied up and held captive even for a short time had shocked her. And she was barely over the events of last night.

It had been fewer than twelve hours since she had caught Skinny and his buddy digging holes in the sundial garden, and when she'd gone to bed after seeing them off the grounds of Castello Serreno, she could never have imagined that she would soon be confronting yet more scoundrels, and that the second set would act in such a way that, this time, the police had *had* to be called.

Now, they had come and gone, and although they'd taken down all the information about what had happened, it was clear to Mallory that they didn't hold out a lot of hope of catching Umberto Mancini, Oliver Price, and Anders Bergmann. They seemed to think that all three of them would be vanishing, never to be seen again. After all, if they *were* caught, they could be charged with attempted abduction, illegal confinement, assault and battery, and something called aggravated menacing. Those charges would put them away for a good long time. Therefore, the police thought they'd be in deep cover and were very skeptical of ever finding them.

Mallory had never been fond of policemen, and the summer before, she'd been happy that none of The Three Investigators' cases she'd been involved with had ended up requiring their services. Therefore, while the police were at Castello Serreno, Mallory had stayed in the background, letting Mrs. Serreno and Jupiter deal with their questions while she took out her laptop and did a bit of research about Anders Bergmann. Ever since he had thrown off his persona as a modest novice monk, she'd been intensely curious about how he or his buddy Price had learned about the Medici treasure to begin with.

In fact, even when his angry red face had appeared in the door of the pantry in which she and the others were hiding, she'd found herself wanting to know the answer to that question – and now she had it. On the genealogical website she'd used to discover Giuseppe Donati's and Alessandro Moretti's ties to the Iluminati, she'd discovered that, although Bergmann had told the truth about his father being Swedish, what he'd neglected to say was that on his mother's side, he had Donati blood.

She'd been bursting with this news ever since she'd discovered it, and now that the cops were finally on their way, and Mrs. Serreno had gone to put Luciano down for his long-delayed nap, she was able to share it with the others.

"He must have heard rumors about the treasure from his family when he was a boy," she said excitedly, "and after he lost all his money and credibility as a hedge fund manager he thought he could start over if he managed to get his hands on a lot of money. He must have brought Price on board because he'd know how to sell the stolen goods."

"How's that?" Bob asked.

"Oliver Price told the truth about having been an accountant," Mallory said, "but conveniently left out the part about going to jail for having been a fence for a gang of thieves who specialized in items of historical interest. He helped them find willing and safe buyers for their goods. He and Bergmann *did* meet in prison."

"Wow!" Pete said. "You found out a lot while we were talking to the police!"

"I know," said Mallory. "I felt a little guilty doing it without the rest of you – or at least without Bob. But once I got started, it would have been really hard to stop."

"That's fine," Bob said. "I should have researched Price long ago myself. Bergmann really didn't seem suspicious to me until this morning."

"He did to me," said Jupiter. "Ever since he made that comment, out of nowhere, about the Russian flu. Anyway, since Mrs. Serreno gave us permission to see if we could open up the secret room, I vote we go there and do that. I don't want to wait any longer."

"Me neither," Pete said.

"Me neither," Bob agreed.

Soon they were back in the conservatory staring at the astrolabe.

"If Jupe's analysis is right," Bob said, "we've got to get the cover off the housing mechanism. But how? At the final moment, Bergmann seemed to have discovered the solution – but we don't know what that solution was."

"I think we can assume," Jupiter said, "that if simple hand tools had been called for, they would have managed to open the room." He squinted and pinched his bottom lip.

It was noon now, Mallory noted, and the sun was overhead. The skylight directed a centered beam of light straight down, and it was surprisingly hot underneath it – even with just one layer of glass petals.

Jupiter noticed the heat, too.

"We have to remember that before Donati and Moretti ever moved into the realm of symbolic dark and light, they first had to bring the treasure over to the United States and transport it across the country. And while I assume it belonged to them, and was perfectly legal, the discovery of what it was would undoubtedly have raised eyebrows. So they had to be extra careful in hiding it in this room we're standing in.

"Even so, they still would have wanted to visit it, probably often, and to be able to get to it easily. The elaborate artifice of the twenty-four glass petals and the fire – that was just for drama and show, something that gave them pleasure, nothing they ever intended to use. So it makes sense that there's an easy way to gain access to the underground room. We just need to find it," Jupiter said.

He climbed over the low stone wall and got to work. Mallory watched as he examined the round wooden cover, looking carefully at its edges. He picked up some pliers and a screwdriver that Bergmann had left, then set them aside.

Mallory watched as Jupiter hunched over the astrolabe. He pointed to the long thin bar that stretched from one side to the other, like the needle of a compass, with its two arrow-tipped ends.

"In a working astrolabe," he said, "this is called the rule, and the astronomer can rotate it to help him with his measurements."

"Does that one move?" Pete asked.

"I didn't think so at first," Jupiter said, "and I really don't know. But I'm afraid of snapping it off."

Carefully he grabbed it near the spot where it rotated around the center and gently twisted. At first, nothing happened, but as Jupiter kept up the pressure, the rule began to move, slowly, and Mallory heard an audible click.

"What was that?" Bob asked. "It sounded like a deadbolt."

Jupiter looked up at them, his forehead

streaming with sweat. "We're getting there," he said. He pointed to the intricate interior circle, with its cutouts and filigrees. "This is called the rete. In a working astrolabe, it rotates too."

Carefully, he inserted his fingers, grabbing one side of the rete, and tried to move it in the direction in which he'd moved the rule. Mallory could see his face grow more pinched, his lips clamping together, a sign he was increasing the pressure.

At last he stood up and mopped his face with a pocket handkerchief.

"No luck," he said. "It's not moving." He looked disappointed. "Maybe it's something else."

"Try rotating it in the opposite direction," Mallory suggested.

Jupiter glanced at her and smiled.

"That's a good suggestion," he said. He bent down over the astrolabe again and grabbed the rete as he had before, but this time, instead of trying to push the carved wooden circle away from him, he pulled it toward him.

Nothing happened.

He looked to Mallory as though he was about to give up, when he suddenly looked at her, light flashing in his eyes.

"And yet it moves," he said. "Eppur si muove!"

Mallory could see a subtle shift in the tension of Jupiter's hand. "Here we go," he said.

Very slowly the rete began to move.

Mallory held her breath, waiting for something to happen. There was another audible noise, like a ratchet clicking. Jupiter kept twisting, and all at once Mallory saw the wooden cover wobble.

"We did it!" Jupiter yelled. "I think the mechanism had just gotten stuck. After all, it hasn't been used in well over a hundred years. I bet it worked a good bit more easily right after it was installed. Can you guys help me lift this off? I want to be careful with it."

Mallory, Bob, and Pete climbed over the stone wall and took their places around the circle.

"O.K.," Jupiter said. "On three."

Mallory had no idea how heavy the wooden cover would be, but she straightened her back and bent her knees slightly.

"One," Jupiter said. "Two. Three."

They all lifted at the same time, very slowly and carefully. It was quite heavy, but they managed to raise it enough to free it.

When it was clear, they placed it carefully on the floor some distance from the stone wall.

When Mallory saw what had been hidden under the cover, she gasped.

"Wow!" Pete said.

Before them lay a stone exactly like the one that Uncle Titus had bought. A thick band of iron had been fastened around its rim to stabilize the stone – which, Mallory realized, wasn't a grindstone at all, but an elaborate part of the mechanism to open the secret room – like the wheel on the door of a safe. It was uncracked and unweathered, and Mallory didn't need a rubbing to reveal the carvings in the stone.

The four moons of Jupiter floated in a large circle of sun, surrounded by a flaming corona. No doubt the design had been created by the three Bavarian families that had founded the splinter sect in Italy, ancestors of Donati and Moretti. And Bergmann. Galileo's birth and death dates were also there.

However, instead of the triangle with the capital letter G in the center – a variant of the Freemason's square and compass – there was a more traditional square and compass surrounding an all-seeing eye of Providence. And while the G still appeared, it now filled the button at the apex of the compass. There was something magical about the surprising variation on this final, working stone.

As Mallory stared at it, the history of the grindstone back in Rocky Beach became clear. That had been the first attempt at the stone circle, but somehow – either in the carving or through some other means – the stone had cracked and it had been discarded. It had lain in the rain and weather for all those years as the sandstone slowly eroded.

Moretti had made another – or had had one of his Italian stonemasons make another, slightly different one. The square hole in the stone's center had been placed over a very heavy square metal rod to which was attached a horizontal metal handle.

Jupiter grabbed the handle and tried to move it. As with the parts of the astrolabe, time had seized up the mechanism. Maybe it was rusted, Mallory thought. But with a screech it began to turn – the iron-banded sandstone wheel turning with it.

A great grinding noise filled the conservatory, and suddenly six of the seven round stones surrounding the well at the room's center began to move. Pete yelped in surprise at the changes nearly under his feet. As Jupiter kept turning, the stones slowly dropped below floor level and then slid back and out of sight beneath the floor itself.

Under them were windows – or skylights in the floor – modeled on the one at the apex of the conservatory's roof, but without the ornate leading and the glass petals – just panes of clear glass that let the sunlight stream through into the underground room.

As Jupiter kept turning, the seventh stone began to drop, and it finally slid back to reveal a cunning spiral staircase, metal steps descending, all arrayed around a central pole.

Mallory was astounded. As if the revelation of the grindstone weren't enough, she was openmouthed at the ingenuity and intricacy of the entrance to the underground room. It was an engineering marvel. And she wasn't the only one who seemed to have been struck speechless. Even Jupiter, not one to be overawed by anything, had nothing to say.

Mallory and Bob stood above the spiral staircase, staring down at the winding stairs, while Pete was on his hands and knees at one of the windows, shading his eyes and trying to get a look down into the room below. Finally Jupiter took charge.

"Who's going first?" he asked. "Pete?"

Pete grinned at Jupiter. "So far so good," he said. "The room looks skeleton-free."

"I'll go first," Bob offered. He bent over, put his hands on the stone floor, and found the first descending step with his foot. He was about halfway down when Mallory started after him.

It was trickier than it looked; every spiral staircase Mallory had ever used had had a winding banister or other support to grab onto. But this was different. She felt she was taking her chances, descending into the unknown.

But by the time she was four steps down, she felt secure. She wrapped her palm around the center pole and let it guide her down. Above her, Jupiter was following her.

When she got to the bottom, she stepped away from the staircase and looked around. What she saw took her breath away. Sunlight streamed down from the windows and the opening in the floor where the spiral staircase was set. Seven shafts of light caught what little dust there was in the air and illuminated it, helping to make the light visible.

Light flooded the room. Like the conservatory, it had a stone floor. It also had stone walls, carefully cut and fitted by hand. Above a circle of stone pillars, gothic arches rose, supporting the weight of the floor and room above. All sound was dampened.

As she looked at the grand array of scientific instruments, each hanging on the wall or resting on its own stone pedestal, Mallory thought of all the museums she had visited. This was a museum, too, of course, but what it most reminded Mallory of was St. Mary's Episcopal Cathedral in Edinburgh. In that soaring space, with its vaulted ceiling, pillars, and arches, she had felt for the very first time the ability of architecture to convey intense and complex realms of emotion.

The room she was in was much smaller, of course, and far less grand, but the feeling it gave her was substantially the same. This was a sacred place. Nothing but the purest motives and intentions had gone into its creation – but the god it worshiped was the god of science.

By this time Pete had joined Mallory and the others, and she looked at his face, alight with wonder. Under normal circumstances, Pete could have been counted on for a wisecrack or a joke – perhaps something more about the absence of Alessandro Moretti's skeleton. But she could see he was as enthralled as she was.

"This is even better than I'd hoped for,"

Mallory said, her voice hushed.

"Come look at this," Jupiter said. He was standing before one of the stone pedestals, and he beckoned for his friends to join him. As Mallory approached, she could see that each of the objects on display had with it a placard with an explanation of its purpose and its origins, written both in Italian and in English.

Mallory found herself looking at an ornate set of calipers, two inch-wide bands of burnished bronze joined together by a circle of bronze at the top, which let the legs of the calipers come together or apart. It was richly engraved with astronomical symbols, and its points resembled claws. A curved rule was bolted to one of the legs, allowing the other leg to slide smoothly over it. It was dated 1599 and its placard read *Calibri nautici, dalla collezione di Ferdinando de Medici. Nautical calipers, from the collection of Ferdinando de Medici.*

"What's it used for?" Pete asked.

"Primarily to measure distances," Jupiter said. "On a map at sea. One point could be placed where you were and the other where you were going, and the distance would show up on that curved rule."

Pete shook his head in amazement and moved on to look at another object. Mallory followed him and soon found herself staring at a beautiful globe of the earth. A brass rod held the globe at a slight angle and was affixed to the back of a turtle, which seemed to be made of solid silver. The placard read *Terrestrial globe, on back of mythological turtle, Italian circa 1620, oak sphere, stained wood, paper, brass, and silver.*

"Why the turtle?" Bob asked.

Amazingly enough, Mallory knew the answer. "I think it must be a kind of elaborate joke," she said. "The ancients believed that the earth was supported on the back of a gigantic turtle. That turtle stood on the back of an even bigger turtle. It was, as they say nowadays, turtles all the way down."

She smiled. She had always thought this idea so ridiculous it was charming – turtles to infinity.

"Is that turtle solid silver?" Pete asked.

"I suspect so," Mallory said. "A rather valuable turtle."

"You can say that again," Pete said.

At some museums Mallory had visited, the sheer number of objects and exhibits on display began, after a while, to meld together, and she'd felt herself grow sleepy as she looked at one thing after another. But the museum in the secret room was totally different. She felt herself grow more and more awake the longer she looked at things.

There were a number of magnificent celestial globes – attempts at mapping the entire night sky on a sphere, with the viewer imaginatively standing at the exact center of the sphere and the universe of stars swirling around him or her.

Though one of the globes was mounted on the back of a horse, they were often contained in wooden stands – four intricately carved legs of dark wood, holding up a wide horizontal circle of metal or wood inside which the celestial globe seemed to float.

One dated from 1085 and had been created by the Muslim astronomer Ibrahim Ibn Said. It was held, vertically and horizontally, by polished bands of brass, with markings to indicate distances. The whole globe rested on a beautifully fitted wooden stand.

"Wow!" Pete said. "Mr. Serreno is going to love this!"

"Yes," Jupiter said. "I think that the Serrenos are going to love everything, but this piece may be of particular interest to them."

"What do you think they'll do with the treasure?" Bob asked.

"I have no idea," Jupiter said, "but I

think they'll make the right decision."

"Maybe it should all go back to Italy," Pete said.

"I see no reason why *that* should be so," Jupiter said. "After all, from everything we've been able to discover, these pieces either belonged to or were legally acquired by the families of Giuseppe Donati and Alessandro Moretti, and they wanted them to come to this country with them."

Mallory hoped that turned out to be true.

There were quadrants of brass and copper, richly engraved, for making astronomical measurements. There were armillary spheres — vastly complicated constructions that looked like circles of metal inside circles of metal, each one representing a planet or star and indicating its movement across the night sky. There were astrolabes, one of which seemed to have a coating of gold leaf that glowed in the light from the six windows as if it burned with an interior flame.

There were also a number of blown glass thermometers that the Medicis had collected. They were beautiful objects, and the placard indicated that they had been made at a famous Italian glassworks.

But Mallory and The Three Investigators were most impressed with the instruments that, according to the placards, had belonged to – or been constructed by – Galileo himself. One entire wall of the room was dedicated to these instruments, and there was a history as well, explaining how Galileo had tutored Cosimo de Medici, and how Cosimo had returned the favor by collecting objects valued by his teacher.

There was a wooden micrometer – a device Galileo invented after he discovered the four moons of Jupiter. He had watched the moons circle the planet and observed that each had a separate and distinct orbit. But how far from Jupiter was each of the moons? He needed an instrument that would accurately measure their proportional distance from the planet.

The micrometer consisted of a wooden ring that could slide up and down the barrel of the telescope, attached to a bar with twelve equal markings. With one eye on Jupiter and its moons through the telescope, and the other on the micrometer's markings, Galileo was able to determine distances based on Jupiter's diameter. It was a simple and elegant instrument, Mallory thought, and a superbly elegant solution to a knotty problem.

There was also a helioscope, an instrument – like the telescope – that Galileo refined, rather than invented, according to the informational card. Since staring at the sun caused blindness, how was an astronomer to study sunspots or flares or other solar phenomena? Galileo decided that the best way would be to recreate the sun's image, so he invented a telescope that projected that image onto a piece of white paper, allowing the astronomer to observe without hurting his eyes.

"Look at this!" Bob said. "This is what got Galileo in so much trouble!"

On a marble stand inside a wooden box with a glass top was a first edition of Galileo's 1632 book *Dialogo sopra i due massimi sistemi del mondo.* The placard translated the title as *Dialogue Concerning the Two Chief World Systems* and described the book as a conversation among three people. One of them advocated the views of Copernicus that the earth revolved around the sun, one was officially neutral, and the third, named "Simplicio," believed that Ptolemy was correct and that the earth was the center of the universe. The very first copy had been presented to Galileo's patron Ferdinando II de Medici. The cover featured a conversation between Aristotle, Copernicus, and Ptolemy.

"It's wonderful what a book can do," Mallory said in wonder. "This book changed the whole world."

She went on to read that the book had been placed on the Index of Forbidden Books, banned in all Catholic countries together with everything else Galileo had ever written or ever might write. The placard said the book had stayed on that list until 1835.

"Yikes!" Pete said. "That book was banned for over two hundred years!"

"People have been banning books ever since there were books," Mallory said. "It makes me so angry. But it's a testament to how powerful they are, and in the end, books always win."

"And here's what started it all," Bob said triumphantly. "One of Galileo's telescopes!"

It stood in the corner, balanced on a marble plinth and extending on either end of it. At first Mallory was astonished that something so valuable seemed to have been placed so haphazardly, but when she got closer, she saw that a channel had been hollowed out and that the telescope rested within it on a piece of dark blue satin.

She was so used to seeing objects behind

glass that she'd been amazed by the fact that, in this room, nothing came between the object and the viewer. If she wanted to, she could reach out and lift Galileo's telescope and peer through it, just as the great man himself had done.

Was it this telescope that he'd looked though when he'd discovered the four moons of Jupiter, or the Medicean stars, as he'd called them? There was no way of knowing, but it was a thrill just imagining it.

It looked quite rudimentary in its satin cradle. It was a tube made of strips of wood, covered with leather, about three feet long — just a handheld device that you could point at the skies while you looked through the other end. The leap forward had come through the objective lens that Galileo had created, in its own separate housing. Mallory was swept with conflicting emotions.

She turned to Jupiter. "It looks so simple," she said.

"It is simple," Jupiter said. "All the best inventions appear that way through hindsight. It's imagining them in the first place that's not so simple."

Mallory thought that was very true. The human imagination was a marvelous thing. In most people all it did was reproduce images that they were already familiar with, creating a world very much like the one they lived in. But for the few radical visionaries, the imagination was a door into a world that had not yet come into being. What if? the visionary asked, and answered that question with a new reality.

But few had upended the world as entirely as Galileo had.

"Is this what you imagined?" Mallory asked Jupiter. She tried to remember what *she* had imagined, and she knew she hadn't come close.

"I wasn't prepared," Jupiter said, "for how emotional it would be."

Mallory nodded. She knew just what Jupiter meant.

16

A Galilean Grindstone

It was two days later, and although Bob had originally told his parents he'd be back in Rocky Beach by now, he wasn't. He and the others were still in the Napa Valley – although they were all staying at Castello Serreno now. There, he sat at a table in the library, his laptop open before him, making some notes about the now-finished case and waiting for the others to get up.

His shoulder still hurt from where he'd been hit with the copper pan, but a lot less than it had when he'd first been hit. He couldn't see it, but Pete had told him he had a bruise on his back that looked a little like the state of Texas, and about as big. It mostly bothered him at night, when he turned over, though it also was a little uncomfortable when he typed.

The last two nights, he and Pete and Jupiter had slept in the room that Oliver Price had vacated – he and Jupiter in the beds, and Pete on a mattress on the floor. Even before Felix had gotten back from Sacramento with Clemente DeLuca and a whole lot of stone,

Fortunata had insisted that the boys move their base of operations from the Mountain Monastery to the house.

After the four of them had emerged from the secret room, they had gone looking for Fortunata, and she had been as thrilled as her husband was, later on, at what they had discovered. Because she was pregnant, she hadn't wanted to risk descending the treacherous spiral staircase, so she hadn't yet seen the wonders in the secret room for herself. However, Felix had.

When he and Clemente DeLuca had gotten back from Sacramento, Fortunata had told him about everything that had happened while he'd been gone, and although her account of the attempted kidnapping of Lucianio made his face go pale, it wasn't long before he was heading into the secret room himself. Clemente DeLuca went with him, and when they walked back into the drawing room where the others were sitting waiting for them, even the normally loquacious and somewhat irreverent Clemente DeLuca seemed to be struck dumb.

As for Felix, he just stared at his wife and his child for the longest time, then gathered them both into his arms. Then he looked at Mallory and The Three Investigators and thanked them eloquently and at length for everything they had done. Right at the moment, Bob was trying to remember exactly what Felix had said, so that he could write the words down in his desktop file, to use when he published his case notes.

He had been typing quickly and surely until he arrived at his memory of this moment. Weirdly, although Bob knew what the gist of Felix's remarks had been, he couldn't remember exactly how he had phrased them.

He knew that Felix had already thanked Pete over and over for his bravery in kicking out the window of the conservatory when he saw Oliver Price grab Luciano − and even more for having the presence of mind to smash the window of the rental van with the poker, distracting Umberto Mancini long enough for him to grab Luciano back from Oliver Price.

Even so, Bob thought that when Felix had emerged from the secret chamber filled with ancient astronomical tools and instruments, he had started his remarks with something else about Pete.

But after that, he had gone on to say that he would be forever grateful to the boys, and to Mallory, for not only discovering these precious relics, but for saving them from those who would have stolen them for money. But how exactly he had said this, Bob couldn't remember.

What he *did* remember – and very clearly – was Felix shaking his head in dismay about the charade Anders Bergmann had engaged in when he pretended to be a man of God. Bob had never believed in God himself, but he had always respected those who did, and he was glad that Anders Bergmann was no longer pretending to be a holy man and had been ejected from the company of the brothers on the mountain.

Not long after Felix and Clemente DeLuca had emerged from the secret room, the stonemason had driven Mallory, Bob, Jupiter and Pete up to the monastery so that The Three Investigators could check out of their rooms and tell Brother Colin or the abbott what had happened.

When they'd arrived, they found the place in a bit of an uproar because Brother Anders had been missing all day and everyone was quite worried. The abbot had returned, and it fell to Jupiter to explain to him that Anders Bergmann wasn't who he'd pretended to be – that he wasn't a *wunderkind* at all, and that he wasn't coming back. As Jupiter had suspected, he and the other monks took the news pretty well.

In fact, they were all very grateful to The Three Investigators for what they had found out about the supposed novice, and the abbott insisted on refunding the money The Three Investigators had paid for their stay at the Mountain Monastery.

He told them that if they ever wanted to come back — perhaps to explore a vocation with the church — they were welcome to stay free for as long as they wanted, and at any time. Though none of them believed they would ever stay in the monastery again, they all thanked him politely. Bob felt a little guilty about how nice the abbot was being when he thought about how he had secretly figured out Brother Anders's ever-changing password and gotten onto the monastery's Wi-Fi.

They said goodbye, but before they left, they took Mallory to see the observatory and also the sundial in the garden. When they ran into Chauncey Kit, he told them that Skinny and his friend had left the campground that morning — and when Pete blurted out that Mallory was Skinny's cousin, Chauncey stared at her in amazement.

"You can't be!" he said. "You're much too pretty! And you don't look anything like him!"

They all laughed at this, then headed back to Castello Serreno. There, Bob and Mallory went to the kitchen pantry to retrieve their cellphones from the ceramic crock of flour into which they'd been dumped, and although they didn't have much hope that the phones would still work, they actually did.

In fact, as soon as Mallory cleaned hers off and turned it on, it rang – and when she flipped it open, it turned out to be Phillipa Paxton. She'd dealt with her responsibilities at the college and was on her way back to the Napa Valley.

She said she'd be there as soon as she could, but Mallory couldn't resist telling her at least the short version of the story, as she stood in the kitchen, a bit of flour on her nose. Phillipa hadn't gotten back to the castle until after dinner, but that evening she and Mallory had gone down to the secret room together, and afterwards had spent a lot of time talking, and it looked to Bob as if they were becoming pretty good friends.

They'd all slept very well the night after the big events, and the next morning Felix,

318

Bob, Mallory, and Phillipa had made a careful inventory of everything in the secret room – after which Phillipa and Felix had started to make phone calls to try to find a temporary home for the Medici and Galilean treasures while they looked for a more permanent home for them. Felix kept saying that he couldn't believe that all this had happened just because he'd sold an old cracked grindstone to Jupiter's uncle. As it turned out, he and Fortunata had decided right away that they wanted to give the instruments to a museum.

A museum in Italy or Portugal? Pete had asked.

No, Felix had said. He and his wife and son were Americans now, and they would give the objects to an American museum. After all, he'd reminded them, Giuseppe Donati and Alessandro Moretti had brought the collection to America. And that's where it should stay.

Of course, it was a little sad to think that the newly discovered secret room would be denuded of its wonders, but they really couldn't keep such unique and valuable objects in a private home. It simply wouldn't be right – though it *was* a pity that the future guests at their hotel wouldn't be able to see the secret room the way its architect had meant it to be seen.

At this, Jupiter had suddenly looked very thoughtful. He turned to Phillipa.

"Am I correct in thinking that museum gift shops frequently sell copies of the things people have seen in the museum – things that people can buy to remember their visit? That although sometimes these copies are simple and inexpensive, sometimes they are what might be called museum quality reproductions?" he said.

"That's true," said Phillipa. "The reproductions can sometimes cost a lot of money, and, to a casual observer, look almost exactly like the original."

Jupiter nodded slowly. "Then I would suggest that you help the Serrenos find a museum that is willing to give them a museum-quality reproduction of every object they donate. Then Felix and Fortunata can put the reproductions back in the secret room, and it would look almost like what we saw when we first went down the spiral staircase."

The Serrenos had been thrilled at this idea – and when Phillipa Paxton said she was absolutely certain she could find not just one, but any number of museums that would agree to this arrangement, the Serrenos ended up hugging one another again.

It was Pete who'd added the perfect final suggestion to this splendid scheme. He said that if the Serrenos made arrangements with a museum within three or four hours of the Napa Valley, they could ask it to put on the informational cards that the collection had been discovered in a secret room in Castello Serreno, and that the hotel had reconstructed the contents of the secret room with replicas which could be seen where they were discovered by patrons of the hotel.

"And maybe even by people who aren't staying here at all!" Felix had exclaimed delightedly. "We could have special tour days when people can come for Victorian high tea, and to see the replica collection!"

"That's a great idea!" Bob had said. "You can put that on your website and use it in your advertising. It will be a great draw for tourists. I bet your hotel will be full all year round."

"Can you imagine how people will feel when Mr. Serreno pulls that lever and those stones move out of the way?" Pete had asked.

"Probably the way we felt," Bob had said. "Thrilled and stupefied!"

It was funny, but he had no problem remembering his own dialogue, he thought, as he wrote it down. But before he could go on entering his memories of the case into his file, he heard a sound behind him and turned to see Pete and Mallory entering the library through the secret passage. He smiled at his friends — and agreed at once when they suggested they all go to the kitchen to get breakfast.

He was getting hungry, and they'd all gotten up so late that Clemente DeLuca and his now-sole assistant were again hard at work unloading the stone they had gotten in Sacramento, while Felix and Fortunata and Luciano had already eaten and were occupied with hotel-related tasks.

According to Pete, both Phillipa and Jupiter were still asleep, but just as Bob was thinking of going and waking Jupiter, he joined them, poured himself some coffee, and got a bowl of cereal.

At breakfast, they ended up talking about Alessandro Moretti's first letter to Brother Benedict — the way it had started with his condolences about how so many monks had been stricken with the Russian flu that the monastery was under quarantine. When Jupiter said that maybe Moretti had simply caught the flu and died of it, Mallory agreed.

"After all, it killed a million people," she said. "Maybe his death just wasn't recorded properly. They didn't always keep the best records back then, and we certainly didn't discover anything to suggest that anyone wanted to harm him or that he died a violent death."

"I'm sorry to think that happened to him," Bob said, "but it does make sense."

Later that morning, they were expecting Worthington to show up to take the four of them back to Rocky Beach, and they now decided to have their traditional debriefing in the library of the castle where their adventure had begun.

"After all," said Bob, after they'd cleaned up from their breakfast and made their way back to the library, "we really should talk about the details of the case while they're still fresh in our minds. And this is great as a place to sit and talk in − a lot better than Headquarters, though I hate to say it, Jupe."

To Bob's surprise, Jupiter looked unruffled at this comment.

"That's actually one of the things I want to talk about this morning," he said, glancing at Mallory. "When we were in the Tower Room the other day, I was thinking about the way Mallory had figured out that the glass petals on the big sundial were the doubles of the glass petals in the conservatory.

"None of the rest of us really noticed the double leading in the skylight, but Mallory's interest in buildings made her look closely, and her precise visual memory made her remember it. Since then, I've been thinking about Pete's suggestion that Mallory design a new Headquarters for The Three Investigators," Jupiter said.

He turned to Mallory. "Would you be willing to do that?" he asked. "We'd keep the old one, obviously, but it would be good if we had a more respectable place to meet with prospective clients, and do research, and even put our mementoes on display. We have enough money in the firm account so that we could pay for whatever materials couldn't be salvaged – and I'm sure my aunt and uncle would let us take a corner of the Salvage Yard that isn't being used for anything else."

"Really?" Mallory asked, her face alight.

"I was thinking you could plan it sometime this summer, and then next spring vacation we could start – "

"To build it!" Pete said.

"I can't think of anything I'd like more," Mallory said. "Thanks so much for asking."

She looked very, very happy.

After a moment she added, "I hate to bring up Skinny, but remember when he came to the Salvage Yard not long after your uncle gave you the grindstone? In his typical obnoxious way he kicked dust and pebbles at it and asked if it was the welcome mat. Nasty as that was, it gave me an idea – I thought if you *did* want a new Headquarters – or a second one – the stone might be its door stoop."

So Mallory had been thinking about this ever since the day the grindstone had arrived, Bob thought.

"But a door stoop can see a lot of wear," Jupiter said, "and the grindstone has already been eroded by the weather. Besides there's the crack. It doesn't look that way, but it's pretty fragile. We wouldn't want it to be damaged by foot traffic. Especially since it's made of sandstone. On the other hand, if it were marble or granite – "

Mallory nodded in agreement.

"Then maybe we could get a marble or granite stoop and the grindstone could be set in a little garden to one side of the entrance," Mallory said. "Or if we really wanted to keep it protected, we could install it inside. I totally agree that there should be a section of the room for the firm's mementos. The grindstone could anchor them."

"That would be great," Jupiter said.

Pete thought so too. "Whatever we do with it, at least we have an amazing memento. In fact, we had a memento before we had a case!"

"That's right," Bob said. "And almost from the start I had a title – *The Mystery of the Galilean Grindstone*. Although, as it turned out, what we thought was a grindstone really wasn't one."

"What do you mean?" Pete asked.

"After I saw what our so-called grindstone really was – a turning wheel for a fancy Victorian Rube Goldberg machine – I looked up the normal dimensions for an actual grindstone, and I found they were thinner and smaller than our stone. Just a little bit smaller, but more than an inch less thick. I couldn't believe I hadn't looked the dimensions up to begin with. If I had, we might have guessed that the stone Uncle Titus brought back from the Napa Valley was even more mysterious than it seemed. We might even have guessed that it was part of a larger mechanical device."

"Not guessed," Jupiter said. "We might have reasoned, or hypothesized. And don't blame yourself, Bob. Uncle Titus told us it was a grindstone, so we all just assumed he was right. We made a very elementary error. In the end, it didn't stop us from unlocking the mystery of Castello Serreno, but we should remember the mistake, and try to avoid it in future."

Bob was relieved that Jupiter was willing to share the blame. He hadn't been looking forward to bringing this up.

"But if it isn't an actual grindstone," Pete suddenly asked, "won't putting a grindstone in the title be misleading?"

Bob's stomach sank. He'd been wondering that himself and was half-sorry Pete had brought it up.

"I don't think so," Mallory said. "For one thing, we all *thought* it was a grindstone until the very end of the case. But even better, if what Uncle Titus brought back to Rocky Beach wasn't a literal grindstone, it would have to be metaphoric, and Bob's titles are *all* metaphors in one way or another. In this case, you could say that if an actual grindstone hones an edge – makes metal sharper – a metaphoric Galilean grindstone is something that sharpens the mind and helps you think."

"I'm not sure I totally get that," Pete said.

"I think Mallory must mean the scientific method," Jupiter said. "The way it makes you ask questions and then more questions, refining as you go."

"Exactly," said Mallory.

"Galileo changed the world with a telescope and a book," Jupiter added. "He may not really have *invented* the scientific method — Felix told us that was actually Ibn al-Haytham, five hundred years before Galileo. But the way he used it eventually let the world see what a terrific tool it was for getting at the truth."

"Yes," Bob agreed, glad that both Mallory and Jupiter were putting into words what he hadn't tried yet to explain, even to himself — though he *had* instinctively understood it.

When the case had just begun, he'd been worried that being dumb about science would get in the way of solving a case involving Galileo. But in the end, it had only required the skills Bob already had. An interest in both history and English could take you a long way in life, Bob thought. This was especially true if you did the best you could to both listen to your own intuitions and also practice the scientific method.

"And you know," he said, "even if Ibn al-Haytham invented the scientific method, and

Mariam al-Astrulabe perfected the astrolabe, I really don't think they'd care much that Galileo is more famous than they are these days. After all, true scientists aren't really interested in fame or money; they're interested in furthering human knowledge. In helping people who *aren't* scientists understand the order that rules the cosmos."

As he said this, Bob suddenly realized that the name that contemplative religious people like Franciscan monks used to describe themselves – an *order* – had been chosen for a reason. Religious people and scientists actually had a lot in common, he reflected. They both believed that doing things – and thinking things – in an orderly fashion, would lead to greater happiness and bigger accomplishments.

It was really pretty ironic that the Catholic Church had accused Galileo of heresy for simply doing the same thing Pope Gregory had done when he ordered a change to the calendar. After all, Pope Gregory and Galileo had, each in his own way, done what they could to fold back the cloak of darkness which for too many centuries before the Enlightenment had blanketed the planet.

But before Bob had time to say this, Jupiter went back to what he'd said about scientists. "That's right," he said. "And the thing about Galileo that makes him someone to emulate is that even though he was put under tremendous pressure to give up his understanding of the way things really worked, he never did."

"Even though he spent the rest of his life under house arrest," Mallory said.

"He stuck to his guns," Pete said.

"Well, I'm glad we seem to agree," said Bob. "Is there anything about the case we're forgetting? I'm going to spend the rest of the morning before Worthington gets here writing up my notes. Did anyone ever call the numbers Anders Bergmann wrote down on the back of the prayer we found in the secret passage?"

"I did," said Jupiter. "And they were just what I thought they'd be. In each case, I heard a sinister voice suggesting I leave a message about the particular goods I was interested in selling. One message mentioned 'rakes,' another 'shovels,' and a third 'hammers' – but in each case, the reference was undoubtedly to stolen – and very hot – antiques."

Jupiter paused and pinched his lower lip. When no one else spoke, he continued. "It never ceases to amaze me that white-collar criminals like Anders Bergmann and Oliver

Price, who branch out into something a little more dangerous and daring, never see a future where they have to make common cause with men who think it's clever to describe hot antiques as rakes and shovels and hammers."

Bob and the others laughed.

"The thing *I* don't get," said Pete, "is why criminals never really seem to *anticipate* stuff. Except in the movies, where they plan those amazing heists. But when I was smashing the window of the van with the poker, I caught a glimpse of Anders Bergmann's face, and he looked surprised more than anything – surprised that his perfect plan was all going wrong!"

"The fact is, a lot of criminals aren't brilliant," said Jupiter almost sadly. "I don't think there are all that many criminal masterminds like Moriarty in the Sherlock Holmes stories. In real life, meticulous thinkers are few and far between."

Just then Fortunata and Luciano came into the library looking for them – or rather, looking for Pete, because, as Fortunata told them, "Pit" was now fixed in Luciano's vocabulary.

When Jupiter and Mallory got to their feet and followed Pete – now carrying Luciano in his arms – Bob went back to the table on which his laptop was resting and sat down in the chair to work. Jupiter had been right. Too many people didn't *think*. To observe things, then ask questions about what you saw, then come up with a reasonable hypothesis was hard work. Or, as Mallory might say, not enough people used the Galilean grindstone.

It was funny, but although the Serrenos' first names all translated into some variation on "fortunate" or "lucky" – and they had certainly been lucky in buying an old calendar house which concealed a Galilean sort of treasure – the truth was, The Three Investigators and Mallory had been very lucky, too, Bob thought.

Their luck had been partly rooted in arriving at Castello Serreno at the right time to catch the villains before they made their move, and partly in Skinny having ripped the vine off the largest sundial while Mallory was there and could figure out what the glass petals actually meant.

Poor Skinny! He'd accidentally helped them when what he'd wanted to do was scoop them by getting to the treasure first. He had absolutely no idea about how to think things through. He'd been driven not by a search for the truth but by arrogance and greed. He had no concept of patience and thought and the careful accumulation of information – and in this case, Skinny's carelessness had been The Three Investigators' luck.

But although, to be honest, *all* of their cases relied on a least a *little* luck, most of them also required what Bob's father liked to call "the application of shoe leather" – by which he meant running around after people and clues – while this one had relied more on what Bob's father liked to call "the use of the old noggin." The old noggin was what Galileo had used, too, when he saw that the grindstone of reality had a way of eventually rubbing false ideas off the surface of the human mind.

Bob typed this idea into his file, but then found himself wondering if the word "noggin" was even a real word. Plugging it into the dictionary/thesaurus he had bookmarked on his laptop, he discovered that it really was. A "noggin" was either a person's head, a small mug or cup, or a small quantity of liquor – typically a quarter of a pint.

This was somehow both peculiar and delightful, and, looking further, Bob saw that the first known use of "noggin" – in the second meaning of the word – was in 1588. Since Galileo had been born in Pisa, in 1564, that meant that the word "noggin" had first been used (in England, Bob assumed) when Galileo was just twenty-four years old. The great scientist and inventor could have sat one evening on the patio of an Italian tavern, drinking a noggin from a noggin while using his noggin to think about the stars.

Maybe he would end his case report with that reflection, Bob thought, smiling to himself – or maybe not. Maybe he'd end it with the observation that, although scientists and religious people could look pretty different from the outside, they both saw themselves as engaged in a lifelong project to improve the condition of humankind.

And although, in recent centuries, scientists had probably done that more effectively than religious people – or for that matter, than historians or writers or even architects – just about every human being was born with some sort of special interest or ability.

If you saw your life as a sort of lifelong scientific project, a project in which you were always collecting data, then using that data to create something useful – and not just for yourself but also for other people – you would probably end up doing your part to build on the work of those who came before you. To keep folding back the cloak of darkness and letting the light in.

In fact, in that way, if in no other, every human being who'd been born since the Enlightenment could be considered at least a potential member of what you might call an invisible but cosmic Illuminati.

Bob nodded and kept typing.

ABOUT THE AUTHORS

Elizabeth Arthur

Elizabeth was born on November 15, 1953 in New York City. She is the daughter of Robert Arthur, the creator of The Three Investigators series. She was educated at Concord Academy in Concord, Massachusetts, the University of Michigan in Ann Arbor, Michigan, Notre Dame University of Nelson, British Columbia, and the University of Victoria in Victoria, British Columbia.

Before she started working on the New Three Investigators series in December of 2018, Elizabeth spent most of her life writing for adults. *Island Sojourn* – a memoir about building a house on a wilderness island in northern Canada – was published in 1980 by Harper and Row. A second memoir, *Looking For The Klondike Stone*, was published by Knopf in 1992. She is also the author of the novels *Beyond the Mountain, Bad Guys, Binding Spell, Antarctic Navigation,* and *Bring Deeps*.

Elizabeth's writing has received fellowships, grants, and awards from the Bread Loaf Writer's Conference, the Ossabaw Island Project, the Vermont Council on the Arts, and the Indiana Arts Commission. She twice received fellowships from the National Endowment for the Arts and was the first novelist ever given an Antarctic Artists and Writers Operational Support Grant from the National Science Foundation.

Her novel *Antarctic Navigation* was chosen by the New York *Times* as a Notable Book, received a Critics' Choice Award from the San Francisco *Review of Books*, and was chosen as a Best Book of 1995 by *A Common Reader*. In 1996 the novel received the Ohioana Book Award for Fiction from the Ohioana Library Association.

Elizabeth has also taught creative writing at Miami University in Oxford, Ohio; the University of Cincinnati; and Indiana University/Purdue University of Indianapolis, where she directed the creative writing program. She and Steven Bauer met in 1980 at the Bread Loaf Writer's Conference and have been married since June of 1982.

Steven Bauer

Steven was born on September 10, 1948 in Newark, New Jersey. He was educated at Hanover Park High School in East Hanover, New Jersey, Trinity College in Hartford, Connecticut, and the University of Massachusetts in Amherst, Massachusetts. In 1970 he received a B.A. with Honors in English from Trinity, and in 1975 he received an M.F.A. in English from the University of Massachusetts.

Steven is the author of three books for young people – *Satyrday*, 1980; *The Strange and Wonderful Tale of Robert McDoodle*, 1999; and *A Cat of a Different Color*, 2000. His book of poems *Daylight Savings* was published by Gibbs Smith in 1989 and won the Peregrine Smith Poetry Prize.

Steven's work has received fellowships from the Bread Loaf Writer's Conference and the Fine Arts Work Center in Provincetown, Massachusetts. In addition, he has been given grants and awards from the American Library Association, the Parents' Choice Foundation, the Ossabaw Island Project, the Massachusetts Arts Council, and the Indiana Arts Commission.

From 1979 to 1982, Steven taught literature and creative writing at Colby College in Waterville, Maine. From 1982 to 2009 he taught at Miami University in Oxford, Ohio where he directed the graduate and undergraduate creative writing programs. In 2010 he established Hollow Tree Literary Services, an independent editing business.